W9-BNG-236

The Trouble With Becoming a Witch

The Trouble With Becoming a Witch

A NOVEL

AMY EDWARDS

BOOK SOLD
NO LONGER R.H.P.L.
PROPERTY

SHE WRITES PRESS

Copyright © Amy Edwards, 2019

All rights reserved. No part of this publication may be reproduced, distributed, or transmitted in any form or by any means, including photocopying, recording, digital scanning, or other electronic or mechanical methods, without the prior written permission of the publisher, except in the case of brief quotations embodied in critical reviews and certain other noncommercial uses permitted by copyright law. For permission requests, please address She Writes Press.

Published 2019
Printed in the United States of America
ISBN: 978-1-63152-405-9
ISBN:. 978-1-63152-406-6
Library of Congress Control Number: 2019907562

For information, address:
She Writes Press
1569 Solano Ave #546
Berkeley, CA 94707

Interior design by Tabitha Lahr

She Writes Press is a division of SparkPoint Studio, LLC.

All company and/or product names may be trade names, logos, trademarks, and/or registered trademarks and are the property of their respective owners.

This is a work of fiction. Names, characters, places, and incidents either are the product of the author's imagination or are used fictitiously. Any resemblance to actual persons, living or dead, is entirely coincidental.

RICHMOND HILL PUBLIC LIBRARY
32972001695818   RH
The trouble with becoming a witch : a no
Dec.. 09, 2019

For my two amazing, light-filled, magical beings, Sidney and Gigi, and for all the other magical ones still becoming their fullest selves.

 # One

BE CAREFUL WHAT YOU WISH FOR.

These words are always with me. I guess because I have found so much truth in them.

As I sit here in the pretty paper gown at the OB-GYN, I know that truth once again, fresh. I wished it. It's hard to accept that I thought something, hoped it, and got it.

If only I were focused on the positive. Is there any positive?

The words just hang there in my head—stuck in front of me, taunting me, saying, "See? It's your fault!"

I hope I have a miscarriage.

Awful, right?

Fuck, I'm awful. But the fight that came right before it is also lingering around, waiting for me to enjoying a rehashing of it too. I am happy to oblige. What the hell, I'm already cold and exposed. Why not add more angst to the mix of self-flagellation? It's a skill I have excelled at over the years—and become quite adept at, I might add.

I can see myself, leaving (escaping?) last night, as I was heading out to the movies with my friend Gin. I offhandedly remarked that my stomach, my just-found-out-I-was-pregnant-last-week-but-was-excited-and-trying-for-it stomach, was hurting.

"If I didn't know better," I said, "I'd think I was going to start my period."

Pete dove right in. "This can't be like last time. You need to really watch your weight this pregnancy."

I was aghast. I think my jaw might have actually dropped. Sure, I got past 180, but I'm tall, nearly 5'9". And I lost it all and weighed less than before now. Is being a size 6 or a size 8 the end of the world? Fuck you.

I can't even remember what I said next, exactly, but it was something like (I'm paraphrasing here), "Stuff it." Or maybe I thought that. I would have enjoyed calling him a motherfucker. I would have enjoyed a lot right then. But I figured the sooner I left, the better.

OK. So, I think I remember—I should remember better, since it was yesterday, but when I get heated I get fuzzy—saying something in my own defense, like, "I think I'll be just fine, and I don't need you telling me that." I recall trying to make it sound delicate, but my tone betrayed my attempt.

Isn't it funny how a situation occurs and then it blurs? I would probably make a terrible detective or crime scene investigator because details always escape me later. This was no exception. I'll attribute it to a mix of anger and annoyance.

I then began making my way across the staid, straight-laid saltillo tile, just wanting to make a break from this person and this conversation. All the while, my stomach was still cramping. I wanted to go sit at the Drafthouse, have a burger or fried pickles or something else comforting, and not feel guilty about it. Let my fat ass be.

"You know," he spouted with a finger pointed my direction, lockstep behind me, "I can't ever say anything to you about your weight."

He didn't used to be like this. It used to be fun and sweet and easy. Now it's pointy and accusatory and weird. It makes me want to run away. I want to see my friend and have someone be nice to me, someone to have fun with.

"That's right. You can't. I don't like it." I opened the garage door, glancing at the hopeful dogs, ears perked, listening for their favorite word: "Out." I shake my head at them and move toward my getaway car, this vehicle of mine just waiting to whisk me away from this annoyance, this person who won't leave me alone right now.

"Well, why can't I? You and I need to be able to talk about this, Veronica!" The finger was wagging and pointing at the same time—a skill he has worked on and perfected over the years. He always likes to point. If you haven't ever been pointed at a lot, you should really try it. It makes it quite a challenge to keep your head on straight and not completely lose your cool. "You need to think about this, and we have to be able to talk about it!"

"No, we don't!" I detected a childlike tone in my voice as I said that. Sometimes I am so glad that fights are not recorded, because we would probably all be so horrified by how we sounded that we would never open our mouths again.

Luckily, I made it to the car. I was in and I clammed up. I hated him right then. I had the thought as he walked back in.

I hope I have a miscarriage. I thought it at that moment.

I went to the bathroom after the movie was over and saw that I had started bleeding.

Now, the one saving grace in this is that the cramps began before I had the thought. Thank God. Or Goddess. Whoever. Just thanks for that morsel. That makes me think that maybe I didn't cause it myself. Maybe my body knew before I did. Maybe some force out there knew before I did. I wanted to have this baby—I did. But as the situation sunk in, I began to question my motives.

I wanted to have another child because I was afraid Annelise might die. Then, I'd have a backup kid. As if she's replaceable.

I wanted to have another child because everyone expected me to. By everyone, I mean the entirety of our families and the whole of the suburbia in which we lived.

I wanted to have another child because thirty-five was looming on the horizon, hanging there, begging to light upon me, with all its advanced maternal age requirements and worries. (Seriously. It's called terribly, advanced maternal age. I guess we should be thankful it's not "geriatric.")

I wanted to have another child because then our kid would have a sibling. I had one, and it's more fun that way, right? Or is it?

I wanted to have another child because I thought I was supposed to. I'm a trigger-puller. I'll just do it. With the infrequent sex we were having at that point in our relationship, somehow my—or his—fertility had pulled it off. It wasn't about love. There wasn't a desire in me to create a bigger family with this man I was supposed to love so much. I just thought I'd get it over with.

I think back to a conversation before this happened. Gin was right. She had told me I wasn't ready. Sometimes a friend sees something in you and you can't see it, and you won't listen. I didn't even understand why someone, even if it was a super-longtime best friend, would say that. Maybe it was our dynamic, Pete and mine; maybe outsiders see things we can't see when we're inside a marriage. I know I have felt like I could diagnose other people's relationships plenty of times. But I didn't listen, of course. She's too harsh with me sometimes anyway, and I tend to ignore it. I didn't listen, and I wouldn't have listened even if she's pushed harder. I did want this baby, when it all boils down. It was still *my baby*.

A knock on the door, and Dr. Nichol is here. Suddenly, the physical pain grabs me hard and won't let go.

 *Two*

A LADY ALWAYS MAKES OTHERS FEEL COMFORTABLE.

So now I'm sad.

Luckily the miscarriage business went fairly smoothly. There wasn't anything weird left hanging around in there. It was early on in the pregnancy, and my body handled everything itself. It hurt, but it wasn't worse than cramps. As the pain started to subside, so did the memory. I tried not to think about it—that, or the stupid fight.

The days and nights pass sluggishly. I resume normal life, and the sadness fades. Taking care of a toddler, feeding her, feeding myself, watching TV, hanging around with my husband, and making life fairly pleasant for all of us. Pleasant and dull.

I spend my days going through the motions. I go to the grocery store. I play internet Scrabble and answer emails and nap. It's pretty easy, and I coast. I'm a coaster. I remember what working life was like, when I had my boutique not so long ago, but I know I am now complacent. We rarely have a sitter, so I only manage to get out with Gin or Xander—someone other than Pete—every once in a while.

Fall has set in, my very favorite time of year. Not that the leaves change much in Texas, but it does go from sweltering to just hot. We can occasionally wear boots without sweating and a light sweater here and there. But it's my favorite time because it always feels like things are changing, like something is blowing in, all mysterious and dark. I love the time change and for it to get darker earlier. It's reminiscent of childhood in some way for me. There was always something in the air in the fall, the impending arrival of holidays and candy and school, friends and boyfriends and football games and something new. That something stuck with me along the way.

I feel excited to introduce Annelise to all these things. I feel excited about making her excited, or something like that. But she's still too little. She gets excited about a new ball or a rock on the ground. The impending mystery and beauty of fall isn't high on her list.

But I can add to the mystery and fun of my own life the simple unfolding of hers and the amazement that will follow as she develops into something and someone that I cannot even imagine.

Then Halloween arrives.

Of course, our plans revolve around this little suburban world, this bubble we live in. I travel daily in a 1.5-mile radius, so my outlook is limited. While I am aware of this fact, I do little to change it. I suppose that mankind has done the same for thousands of years, and that basic rationalization gets me partway through it. Or maybe not. Perhaps the traveling and wandering nature of my humanity is being suppressed. Whatever the case, I am ignoring it and trying to pay my bills with what little money we have. I'm trying to just live my days and essentially keep my child alive and content and have sex with my husband every so often, even though it's a total chore to get myself going on that front most of the time. Sad but true.

We plan to head down to a neighboring home for a little get-together, where the kids can play and the parents can show off how their kid is the cutest in whatever costume they have cooked up. There are probably twenty kids on our street alone, all under the age of four. It seems like this is where I am supposed to be, because everyone else is here, so yeah. I do it. The mom thing, the suburban thing, the this-is-what-you're-supposed-to-be-doing thing.

Sometimes I think that I should get a minivan. But that disturbs me on some level, like then I have really lost some battle, even though I don't know that there is a battle going on. It is disturbing because I think there's a stigma attached. I feel as if I have become the cliché minivan-mom and then I am, officially, UNSEXY MOM. I might as well wear a sign. And, *I like sexy*. At least, I used to. I surely don't have a problem with moms in general. I liked my own mom, yes; but I have focused on liking sexy for a huge chunk of my life. I think it's integral to our nature as women. I am not sure what happens once a woman loses her sense of sexiness, but

I have slipped over to that side on occasion. It snowballs into a self-esteem nightmare of food and derisive, hurtful, internal chatter. Maybe that's just me. Maybe a woman can just shut down—just turn it off and go with all the other labels that make up a complete woman—without that one sexy part mixed in there. Take a selfie at the right angle and get some likes on Facebook, and that'll get you through. For some reason, I suspect that I will find all this out the older I get. But I hope that sexiness is a state of mind. I fucking want to hold onto it, keep it firmly in my grasp, and know that it's there warming my palm, even if no one ever sees it and no one but me ever knows it's there.

On this Halloween, I certainly don't go the slutty route, as many a young woman is apt to do. But I do try to at least incorporate a microbe of sexiness to my outfit of all black (slimming!) with cat ears on my head. Original, eh? And, of course, Annelise looks the cutest in her little ladybug outfit. All the other mothers will fawn over her as I show her off like a doll. Not really. But I think she's comfortable, and she really does look sweet as she barely toddles along.

I fielded the daily and incessant questions from Pete: *Are you sure you should wait to bathe her? Is she going to bed late? Is that a good idea? Are those the right shoes for that outfit? Can she wear that without being itchy? Did you bring her something to drink? What should I wear?* Good god. For someone so uninvolved, he sure wants answers all the time.

The air swirls down the cul-de-sac, into the house, swinging open wide the beveled glass front door. We block the dogs from getting past us and hauling ass down the driveway and into suburban oblivion. Dusk has fallen, and Annie is up late (most parents around here work). She's fed but happy, and she's ready to shove chocolate in her mouth, sporting what I think are the right little black, sparkly, most ladybug-esque shoes.

We head down eight houses to Kathy and Mark's, for food and general Halloween small talk. Pete has already not cooperated with me, and I had to manage to get everything done myself while he last-minute got the yard trimmed and then had to shower, which takes way too long. I am annoyed because the yard could have been done hours ago. Lack of advance planning is a thorn in my side. Yes, people will walk by our yard, but does it really matter?

But I "whatever" that right out of me. *Whatever, let's just go, and see if I fuck you tonight, because the likelihood of that is shrinking by the second unless you actually help put the baby to bed without being asked and let me rest, because it's not like you work that much anyway, and maybe I do have some anger issues I am suppressing, but all is fine right now, or it damn well looks like it is as we stroll the sidewalk of our perfect happy neighborhood.*

Decorations abound, and children are beginning to go trick-or-treating. Several neighbors are already out remarking on how cute Annie looks. I gladly accept the praise and take credit in a surprised-as-Taylor-Swift "Who me? Thank you, thank you!" kind of way. We decide to go ahead and let Annie trick-or-treat some before going to our friends' house. We take a video of her starting to walk up to a door, but she seems confused and nervous. Pete pipes up. "Make sure she holds her bucket."

I'm like, what? So, I say, "What?"

"She needs to hold her candy bucket."

Um, this child can barely walk. He has his camera out, and I figure he wants her on video walking up to her first house, jack-o-lantern bucket in hand. I wonder if I'm in the shot. I wonder if I look fat. I wore black for a reason, but sometimes, it's sneaky.

My focus shifts to the little ladybug before me. "Sweetie, here's your bucket, hold on to it so you can get your goodies!"

She takes it in her hand and promptly drops it.

I pick it back up and put it in her hand.

She gets a good grasp on it this time and seems confident. She takes one step, trips on nothing, and falls face forward, bucket flailing flat out in front of her. She starts to cry.

So, of course, I want her to stand up and keep going. I think Pete is rolling the vid right now too, beer in the other hand. But Annie seems nervous again and senses that something is expected of her. She has an audience. She continues to cry but it begins to dwindle down to a low whimper. She wants me to pick her up. It's late for her little baby body. I pick her up, pick the bucket up, and head for the front door so she can ring the bell.

"Put her down so she can walk up with her bucket."

Seriously? I sigh an annoyed sigh, making sure that it's just loud enough that Pete can hear it, with just enough tiredness in it to drive home my point. A sigh can say a thousand words.

She starts to cry again as I hand her the bucket.

"Well, now you've picked her up once so that's what she wants."

"Why does it matter?" Two sets of parents and three kids are getting closer to us from the street, ready to hit this house. Of course, we know the families.

I feel pressure. Pressure to look the part. We have one of the biggest houses on this street, thanks to some money my parents contributed, and in the little 'hood we're in, I always feel some pressure to set some kind of happy family example. That's probably twisted in lots of ways. A good example—the best example—would be a family that's real, warts and all. No dark underbelly lurking around. Plus, I hate to make others feel uncomfortable. My mother once told me long ago that a true lady is someone who always makes others feel comfortable and welcome. But even before she said that, my dislike of conflict and my desire to avoid it led me squarely in that direction. Keep everyone happy. Be sweet. I fail miserably sometimes. But trying counts, right?

Small tunnels of light from flashlights in kid hands continue toward us. Annie cries some more. I pick her up.

"Well, V," he says in a subdued, controlled anger voice that edges on condescending, "I was trying to get the first house she walked up to on video for us." He is speaking so slowly that it's almost offensive, and the tone is what you might hear someone using with a person who just got their order wrong. It was a tone of perceived incompetence, as if I didn't know the plan. Annie is silent now.

"Yeah, I know. But I'll just help her along, and we can get that, right?"

His turn to sigh. I think about how this is so stupid, that we are both so silently fuming about such a silly thing. But that's how I roll, how I fight. Or rather, how I *don't* fight. I keep it in, keep it in; I don't want to go there. I am a terrible fighter. I can only think of the things I want to say about two days too late.

His sigh says anger. It is terse enough to say to me, "Oh, how difficult it is to deal with stupidity." It is long enough to let me know that he's exasperated. And it's loud enough to let me know that I was completely supposed to hear it, to catch every inflection and meaning.

The other parents are right upon us. I say hi to everybody and thanks for remarking how cute Annie is. Pete puts it right on. *All* on. He's so happy, he thinks everyone is the cutest. I am sure that my girlfriends, Bonnie and Meg, think that I am so lucky, that he's so gregarious and fun, and we are having a great time, and aren't we the picture of what life should be. Or maybe they see straight through us and that we are big fakers.

"Are they home?" Joe, another dad in the mix, asks about the house we're camped in front of.

"Annie dropped her bucket, so we haven't gone yet." I nod while explaining. "A small bucket incident!"

Everyone chuckles and says how that's OK to little Annelise. Even though what I said wasn't funny, they play along, since I was attempting to sound light and fun.

"Oh, well now I can get everybody going up together!" exclaims my husband, the master transformer. Fine. I'll file that in my "whatever" folder. I carry Annie toward the door. She says, "Down," so I put her down. I hold her hand and try the bucket in her other, and she takes it. I glance back at Pete, but he isn't looking at me. He's just looking smugly at his phone and his video.

She does great and even tries to say "Trick or treat?" with all the other kids, which we had worked on this morning. We get candy from the neighbors—the only ones I don't really know. They are some retired couple (not my idea of a great retirement, surrounded by children in suburbia—I am instantly suspicious), but maybe they're there for resale value. We wrap up house number one when I say to Pete, "See? She ended up doing great! That didn't even matter."

"No, V," he says, using his slow, controlled, annoyed, having to deal with an idiot voice, but low enough so it's obviously meant for me and me alone. "*You* think it didn't matter."

Other people can hear us.

"Oh my god." I stretch that out long enough with a baleful expression that lets him know that these little tiffs are exhausting. In case he didn't get it, I go ahead and spit it out, letting it ring quietly loud and clear. I walk away as I utter, "You're exhausting me."

I putter away toward another house and start talking to Bonnie. She's cool.

"How's work going?"

"Oh, pretty good," she says with a sigh as her three-year-old, Liam, runs ahead and out into the street. "I have papers to grade this weekend and the UT faculty is running a special lecture series on the economy, so a lot of the professors are going to that since it's coming up. But other than that, I'm just managing, you know."

I nod along. "Oh, that's cool." I'm hiding the fact that I am totally jealous. She's a University of Texas law professor. Sometimes I wonder why she lives in a suburb like Circle C, all planned development and all. She's got two kids, a law degree, and a prestigious career at a fantastic law school. Why don't they live somewhere way cooler than this? Or, wait—is *this* cool to some people?

We make small talk as we stroll and look after the kids. Luckily, Pete is doing the same. I am glad because then he won't try to tell me what to do. I open a package of gummy Life Savers for Annie. She is thrilled.

"Should she be eating that?" Pete has come up behind me, surprising me with a question.

"Why not?"

"Well, I don't know, just cause she's little and I'm not sure that's a good idea."

I sigh. Lots of sighing. I stop and turn to him. "You know, Pete, either take it away from her or trust me. Seriously. I am not trying to harm our daughter." People are walking away from us. I can tell they are pretending not to listen.

"Look, I know you're not. I just want to make sure that it's OK, that we make sure not to give her stuff she can't handle."

Oh, the tedium. Always the questions. "Believe it or not, Pete, I do actually think about things before I do them." My hands go up in surrender. "I am not just doing . . . whatever . . . and oblivious . . . to facts, or to Annie." Maybe I'm the bitch. Maybe I am just a big ol' bitch all the time. But I get really tired of being questioned by him. It's like he doesn't want to trust me. "Just stop asking me questions all the time." I kind of can't believe that I just blurted that out.

He gives his incredulous laugh of disbelief. He should copyright that. He's perfected it. "Don't you think I am just trying to know what's best for Annie?"

"That's another question." I know I am just being belligerent, but I don't care. The other couples and kids have moved on to the next house and are ringing the doorbell. They know we're having words. Tense words. Annie is still involved with her candy, and that's good, because I feel really bad when she hears us argue. But she seems oblivious. I hope she really is. I worry about that. This can't be good for her.

That thought makes me soften. Quickly, I add, "I'm sorry. I didn't mean that to come out all bitchy." My gaze falls to Annie. "I know you do. It just seems like you don't trust me when you are constantly questioning every decision I make."

But I have already lit this fire, and it can't be put out that easily. Pete turns it around on me and pulls out the old pointer-finger with it. "You know, V," he's in my face now, close enough that I can smell the beer on his breath and see the glint in his eyes, "I *don't* trust you. Not all the time with her."

My shoulders slump and I look at my feet. I see the sweet blades of grass peeping over the lawn and onto the curb. I wish I were a blade of grass. I wish I were anywhere but here. Some of our other friends from across the street, Dave and Kim and their two-year-old daughter Laura, start to approach us.

"Why not?" I hear the sadness in my voice. When Annelise was only a few months old, and I was trying to adjust to the demands of motherhood and breastfeeding and an incessantly demanding little life-force that commandeered every aspect of our lives (or so it seemed), I confessed to Pete that sometimes I just felt like throwing the baby across the room. He was horrified.

I didn't mean that I actually ever would, I tried to explain, but just that I felt it. I had told my sister-in-law the same thing, and she had understood. Of course, she's a mom. All she said was, compassionately, "Sure you feel that! But you don't do it."

I thought Pete would understand. He proceeded to go on and tell me how I had changed, and he pointed at me. I went and sat in the closet. Great solution, I know. I might as well have curled into the fetal position and hidden in a hole.

But now, more neighbors, more *fun!* Dave, Kim, and Laura are walking up, and they are close. Our girls barely acknowledge each other. But Pete keeps up an appearance. His entire demeanor shifts.

"Hi!" he states largely. "Oh my gosh! Laura, you look sooooooo beauuuuuutiful!" Laura is dressed up as a bumblebee with a wand. Fine. That was the end of that discussion. I'll play along. I perk right up. Ever the lady.

We make it to the party, and it's fun enough. Talking to Bonnie is a breath of fresh air in a world of conversations revolving around sippy cups, kids' illnesses, and, the favorite, "guess what new cute thing (insert child's name) did!" I overhear Pete talking about his deer hunting trip set for the next day, the start of hunting season. I'll get a break from football and hunting and, well, *him* for the rest of the weekend.

I have had two glasses of wine and all looks better in the world—or, shall I clarify, in *my* world. Things do usually look better through cabernet-colored glasses. Annie is getting tired. She's starting to fuss now and then, between things I shove in front of her to eat and little toys she finds scattered about that hold her interest. I pick her up and go find Pete in a conversation about, I am sure, something very manly or very Republican (is there a difference?) that he is involved in with a couple of other guys.

"Hey."

"Hey."

"Sorry to interrupt, guys." I give my sweetest smile, the demure version. "I'm gonna take little one here on home. It's time."

"Oh, she needs to go?"

"Yeah." I then give the universal hand wave that says, "no problem." "But you can totally stay. I'll get her to bed. I'll just see you in a little bit."

Pete starts to stand up. "No, I'll come, too." The other guys are looking at us.

"No, seriously, babe, stay! I'll take her home, and you can stay and have fun." I meant every word. I think I sound convincing. If the situation were reversed, I'd be cool with that.

Pete looks at me and nods and speaks slowly. He raises his eyebrows and says, "No, I'm going to come with you."

Please don't. "Oh, OK. I just wanted to let you know it was OK to stay if you wanted."

"Just let me say goodbye."

"OK. I've already told everybody bye, so I'll just start walking and you meet up with me." By this point, I have made it to about five paces from the front door. Annie is so tired she's ticking, ready to go off, and she still needs a bath. I can see the chocolate embedded in her fingernails and the crumbs under her red and black ladybug collar.

"Can't you just wait a minute while I say goodbye?" His voice is slow and determined, like I don't understand.

"Why don't you just stay for a little bit, finish your beer, and say bye? And I'll get going and see you in a few?"

"V! Why are you telling me to stay? I don't want to stay!" This tone. It's like yelling, but conducted in a low, controlled voice. I marvel at how that is even possible, but it is.

"Oh my god! Then come on!" I turn on my heel and head for the door. He goes the other direction, and Dave and Kim are right there to say goodbye.

I manage another bye and thanks tossed their direction, for about the tenth time. Pete is in character, shaking hands and being generally overly enthusiastic. I hear the words wonderful and fantastic being thrown around, and I feel disgusted. It's gross. I can't listen anymore. I open the door and walk out with my own smile, very real, because I want to get away from him and people and the tension between us. It's palpable and stifling and suffocating and constant. I can't wait for him to leave tomorrow—leave, and let me have the comfort.

 *Three*

TEACH YOUR CHILDREN WELL.

It's Halloween night, and I can't sleep. This house is big and quiet, and the dogs are snoring a little at the side of the bed. Pete is sleeping after watching TV—some old Will Smith stinker of a movie that he watched for the fiftieth time. I was guilty, too, though. I watched *The Craft* for about the eightieth time, and I still love it. I love movies or TV shows or *anything* about witches. The subject holds a lot of fascination for me.

But I have been scared of that subject, too. Protestant upbringing makes you fear the worst. Even though these days I don't believe in hell, I am still held back from studying any sort of "witchcraft" because, well, what if someone found out? What would they think? They'd think I was going to hell and that I am an evil person, surely. And maybe they would be right—dabbling in the unsavory world of the *dark arts!*

But here I am, lying in bed thinking about that movie. I like best the part when the four girls become actualized witches. They all band together, look all hot, and have cool powers, and each one gets something in her life that she has been wanting really badly: one gets money, one love, one talent, and the other beauty.

I want something.

I want *lots* of somethings.

I creep out of bed, grabbing the baby monitor, and try not to wake the dogs and the husband. I internally harrumph at the husband part. My heart isn't in it anymore. My heart isn't soft toward him. I remember that it used to be, but that was eleven years ago. I think that my eyes were full of stars, and I thought that opposites really did attract. Now, I'm not so sure. Instead, I just want opposites to *accept*, and I don't feel accepted or trusted. This child changed everything.

I go to where my phone is charging and check it. It's not plugged in right. It's dead. Ugh. I re-plug it in and form a Plan B. I hear Poppy, our terrier, raise her head in curiosity and listen. She may join me.

The house is dark, but I make my way through, guided by many nights of getting up for a crying baby. I traverse the Berber carpeting of the downstairs and head through the living room. I go up the stairs and into Pete's office, mess that it is, with papers, unopened envelopes, and Post-it notes with one cryptic line scratched down on each. I have cleaned and organized this office repeatedly to no avail. I do it not only for my own neat-freakishness but thinking too that maybe then he'll earn some money by knowing where his things are.

I step over to the computer and give the mouse a shake. The monitor rustles to life. I close the internet browser, now set on some page with mortgage quotes and another tab with monkeys you can dress in all different outfits and send to your friends and start fresh. I kinda want to try the monkeys, though, and have a moment of regret about closing that one.

OK. Fingers poised over the keyboard, I start googling. *The Craft*, craft spells, witch spells— I am led down many different paths. I can't remember a time in my life when I wasn't wondering about the moon, or the sky, or how I suspected I could feel what was happening with others even when no words were said. My mother, a devout Christian, used to tell me I was a healer and that I only needed to "lay hands" on someone to help them heal. How does a five-year-old process that? Probably by thinking it's a sort of magic. I guess I can't remember thinking anything other than a general, *Doesn't everybody sense a feeling in a room, an energy?* That's so natural to me that it never occurred to me to truly question it. I just accepted it, and then went to the Methodist church with my mom and dad and sang, "Jesus loves me," with the other kids.

My hand goes to the center of my forehead, and I sit for a moment. I look back to the computer, and I google "spell to change your life." Oh my god! Did you know that people—witches, I guess—actually charge online for their spells? They're pricey, too! I discover this because there's a spell for love, wealth, revenge, binding, windfall, weight loss, attraction, and happiness (tall order!)—that one will run ya $399. I don't know why I'm so surprised. Something about that just seems wrong to me. I keep poking: how to spell, how to cast a spell. There are a lot of rabbit holes. I find a site that's free that centers on change. My mind flashes to the miscarriage. That was certainly something that changed. I shake it off. I want to read more, but I've gotta pee.

I slink out of the office, pull the door behind me slightly, and head into the hallway, past Annie's room. The bathroom is really cold, and my feet make a sticking sound as they meet with the cool, cheap, white vinyl masquerading as tile. Brrr. Quick as I can, I am back up, and after a quick glance in the mirror, I turn up my nose at the reflection of dark hair messily piled high and bright, awake, brown eyes. I head back to the office. The door is standing wide open. Weird.

I slowly press it open, and there's Pete, at the computer, checking it all out. I probably have five tabs open and have been at this for like twenty-five minutes, so it wouldn't take a computer whiz (which he is not) to click the back arrow a few times and see just what I have been researching.

He looks up at me with a grimace. I try a cute little no-teeth smile.

"What are you doing up here?" he asks.

"Just messing around on the computer." My instinct is to downplay this. But maybe it won't matter.

"Looking up . . . *witch* stuff?" He dragged out the word *witch*. I detect condescension. Great.

"I was watching *The Craft* on TV, and it was just on my mind. I was just looking. I guess cause it's Halloween and everything, too!" I give a little, light chuckle and a one shoulder shrug.

"I don't really want you looking at this."

"I was just looking." Defensive tone detected. Oops.

"I know you've always wanted to be a witch." Dripping with condescension, he keeps going. "But I don't think it's right to have this in the house. Not with Annie."

"Right . . . because she's so good at reading what's on the computer? A child prodigy."

"V, I don't want it in my house."

Ooh, I'm biting my tongue. Bite, bite, bite! *Your* house? It's not half *mine?* Or more, if we want to get technical, considering that I (or my dad, anyway) made the entire $50,000 down payment and that each month's payment is from my (or what my dad set up for me) rental income? OK, so if we're getting truly technical, maybe it's more my dad's than anyone else's, but with him gone now, doesn't that fall to me? Tongue. Bitten. And why is this such a big deal? I might as well have had a pentagram on my forehead.

I'm quiet. I don't know what to say. I just want to look, to explore the ideas. To see what it says. I keep my mouth shut.

"And I don't want you teaching our daughter what you believe."

I stare in hurt disbelief and tilt my head while a little sigh escapes my nose.

Guilt and blame wash over me, each taking turns with their waves. This is all my doing. I've never taken the time to stand up for myself. Once, when Pete and I were first dating, and things were so easy and blissful and happy, I remember riding in his old burgundy two-door Honda coupe together. The windows were down and the early warmth of springtime in Austin blew all around us, whipping my hair into my mouth so I'd have to pull it out of my gum sometimes. I had been thinking about how Pete was raised, how I was raised, and how, during college, I had longed for ways to find more openness in my thinking about religion and spirituality. I had trouble finding it, but I knew that something lay dormant within me.

I blurted out, as I sometimes do when things are pent up for too long, "You know, I'm never going to believe what you believe."

He looked at me with mild surprise—more surprise that I was talking about this than about the meaning of the comment itself. He gave a relaxed and easy half-shrug with the shoulder nearest me, and said, "yeah, that's fine." And he leaned over and gave me a kiss.

Now, I don't know what he thought that meant. I wonder sometimes if he knows me at all. Was I never clear? It's my own fault. I wasn't clear. Look at my family, my life, my history. It's by the book. It's what it's supposed to be. Why would he think anything else?

And yet, he seems to know now. Which makes me think he knew all along.

I brought more confusion and blame onto myself by agreeing to raise Annie as a Catholic. I did. I was like, *Oh, it'll be fine.* With the deep desire, all along, that I would teach her exactly what I thought, too. That was Catholic *enough* for me.

He continues, eyebrows raised, and lays it out for me, to get it through my head. "No, V, we agreed when we got married to raise her Catholic. You made a promise."

That's true, I did. My father had impressed upon me to take that decision seriously—that's why it was on my mind in the car that day. He said, "Veronica, you're dating him. If it's serious, you need to think about your kids, because Catholics expect you to raise your kids Catholic." Apparently he knew how seriously Catholics take that shit. Sorry. That *stuff.* What did I do, at twenty-four? Exactly the opposite—I didn't take it seriously. I thought, *Well, my fiancé and two best friends were brought up Catholic, and they all turned out great, so what the hell?* I thought, *My dad is a different generation—things aren't like that anymore. It'll be fine, and on the side, I will teach our children all the additional things I believe.* Like, for example, things I did manage to learn in college—like how the Bible had a gazillion authors and isn't full of factual details; like how I think there can be truth and beauty in all religions; like how I don't think there is a hell or a horned devil waiting to pitchfork us in the butt and throw us into an actual fiery inferno. Just to name a few.

I turned to Pete. "Aren't the things I believe part of what you love about me?"

"That's not what this is about."

I note that that wasn't a yes or a no. Avoiding the question much?

"It's about you teaching our daughter what you and I agreed on, that we would raise her Catholic, and that's important to me. I just don't want you teaching her anything like this."

I bet the trust issue from earlier tonight is in here again. Now he feels like he can't trust me to not teach her this stuff, to not tell her whatever I want. He's right. He can't trust me on this. I just want to avoid this, to avoid the fact that he would rather live this so-called "right" and religious way, than to accept who I am and let me be who I want to be. I feel defeated. I surrender to this conversation and this conflict, not wanting it, but knowing deep down that I will still, someday, teach my daughter whatever I want.

I don't agree, and yet, I don't fight it. "Just close it up. I'm going back to bed." I *so* don't want to sleep next to him right now, not at all. I turn and walk away, fully ready to get the hell away from this conversation and this person who I feel stifled by. Ugh.

I am still not asleep when he comes in the room to go to bed as well. He hears me stir.

"I want to go to church on Sunday."

I lightly sigh and close my eyes.

 *Four*

NOTHING VENTURED, NOTHING GAINED.

Good god. Getting me to go to church has always been like pulling teeth. I have never liked it much. I get bored, so bored. I remember back in my slightly slutty high school days, I would use the sermon, a long prayer, or whatever time spent just sitting there to mull over my make-out or sex session from the night before, pondering whatever guy I was currently hooked on. Even when I was a young kid, there was a time that I sat and cracked all the knuckles of my toes during a service. When another woman in church laughed about seeing that to my mom, who had been standing and hadn't seen me, my mother was absolutely horrified. But taking it further was the ritual within the space that always dragged on and on. There was nothing magical or special there. It seemed stale and rote. What spoke to my heart event then was being out-side, nature, friends, and love.

Now I try to listen, but I end up daydreaming, off in space, every time. Feeling that same dull staleness that seems to be so easily accepted as comforting. Maybe I should think up a spell today. I might burst into flames.

I survive church for two reasons. First, because of Annie, we get to be in the back, behind the glass with all the other parents and little kids. She toddles around while we try to keep her fairly quiet. It's great. I hardly have to pay attention at all. Second, Pete is always running remarkably late. We never arrive until the service is about a third of the way in. It's the one time that I love his lateness. I encourage it and do nothing to stop it on these churching occasions, which are few and far between, thank God or Goddess or whoever.

Done with church and headed home, I am grateful that I can just focus on Annie, on feeding her lunch and getting her down for a nap. Pete will be packing for his deer hunting excursion and then heading off to South Texas to go kill things. Ick. But good.

I text Gin.

Hey. Pete leaving in a while till Wed. What are you doing today? Call me later.

I need a friend to talk to today. I am feeling too stifled and stuffed and generally ill at ease about my life. Something is missing, something big, like connection and love. Can connection fade out? Can you have had it and it goes away?

Duh. It can fade. I know that I have formed tight friendships with people only to have them fade so quickly when the experience was over. I am thinking particularly about camp, years ago, when I became instant best friends with the coolest girl, Steph. We were inseparable for that month and loved each other so. The thought of ever not being friends seemed impossible. But then we went back to our regular lives and realized that we were quite different and lived three hours apart, which only exacerbated the problem. Our connection wasn't there anymore, and we drifted right apart. I wonder where she is now. I've looked on Facebook but can't find her. We probably wouldn't be close anyway. It'd probably be awkward. She probably wouldn't even care anymore. I don't care. Who the fuck cares. Just something to waste time. Boy, am I negative today.

I am ready to get home and put Annie down for a nap, and Pete says he's almost ready to go. That probably means another hour of him here, unfortunately. I can't wait for him to go. It's probably very wrong that I am this excited. My home—*our* home—feels more at peace when he's not here. I can relax, and I don't feel this constant tension. Did we always have this, and I didn't notice? Maybe. I don't know. All I know is that now I want him *away*. I want to kick back tonight, get Annie in bed, veg out, have a martini or some wine, maybe have Gin or Xander come over, maybe smoke a little weed, chill. All good. All escape. I am trying to hide that I want him gone by being sweet and helpful.

Annie's in bed. I am milling around, asking Pete if he needs anything, expediting this departure. It finally happens. I peck him on the lips and smile and wish him lots of happy hunting.

I go straight in and call Gin.

"Hey!"

"Hey." She never sounds excited. Always the same, collected tone.

"What're you doing?"

"We just got back from church, and now Tim's all fired up about the Titans game."

"Yeah? I went to church, too. Now Pete's gone to Mike's ranch for a few days."

"Oh yeah, deer season starts tomorrow."

"Yep."

Silence for a moment.

"I'm glad he's gone," I say.

"Really? Why?" She genuinely sounds surprised and confused.

"Ummm . . . I don't know. I just feel like you and Tim have the best, easiest relationship. I'm just sick of Pete. All we did was pick at each other when we were out trick-or-treating with Annie, and that developed into little, like, fights, and it was just like one thing after another. Then we'd both put on this happy family face to all our neighbors. It just seemed so fake and stupid."

"You know what, V? Ever since seventh grade you've been like that. You don't want to make other people uncomfortable. That's not bad. But it's OK to make other people uncomfortable once in a while. Who fucking cares? You're just saying how you feel. They can take it. But Pete does it for a different reason."

"He does?" I need reassurance.

"He just wants to look like this person who has it all together when he isn't even really working or doing anything. He just puts on this face and this way about him, and, lemme tell you something, people can tell. Tim's dad totally saw that the first time he met Pete. I mean, I love Pete and I don't mean to say anything bad, but he likes to . . ." Gin pauses as she backpedals, which she tends to do, out of fear of saying something too negative or being responsible for someone else's actions. She adds, "He likes to just be this image he has in his head, and he likes for you and Annie to be it, too."

"Yeah. I guess that's right."

"It is right."

Period. She's so sure. I love that about her. She manages it in a non-judgmental way that works. "So do you want to come over tonight?"

"I don't know. This is the only night that Tim has off, so I want to hang out with him. We want to go somewhere we can watch all the games for our fantasy."

Fantasy Football. Navigating football season with them is always a challenge.

Then she says, "Why don't you come out here and bring Annie?"

"Eh. Maybe. I just want to chill here though, with Pete gone, and be in my house all peaceful and quiet tonight and have a drink and sit around and veg."

"Yeah, I understand. Well, let me know if you change your mind."

I hang up and scratch my head. I sit and stare out the window, past the plants on the window sill and into the backyard, through the ugly privacy fence that barely provides any privacy we can see straight to the house behind us, which the voyeur in me loves to do. There's something about seeing a house from the outside that is just so cozy and warm to me, especially when it's lit up at night and you can see in. Sometimes, looking at things from afar is so much better than actually being in them.

I learned this about carnivals when I was little. I used to think I had to go. I would see all the lights from afar and the Ferris wheel beckoning to be ridden with all its twinkling circular glory, but then, when my parents would finally give in to the begging and take me, it was never as good as it had looked from the car at dusk on that faraway hill. It was dusty and dirty, the people didn't seem to care much, and the rusted rides creaked and moaned under the pressure to perform yet again. So, the ideal home life is right there, staring back at me as I play Peeping Tom, thinking everything is perfect and wonderful and apple pie, when really he may be having an affair and the countertops may be a mess and the floor filthy and the kids crying and the bills not paid and the trash stinks. But it's great from the outside. It can be anything I want it to be.

I snap out of it. Baby's gonna be up too soon. I should call while I can.

I call Xander. Turns out he's gotta leave for New York tomorrow morning, early, and I feel a pang of jealousy. I remember traveling. I remember New York. I had my little boutique and used to go and buy. It feels like a lifetime ago now. I want to go there. Pang, pang.

Maybe it's a sign that I should be on my own tonight. I want to go to New York.

I have simultaneous pains of *I want* and *I don't want*. I want everything. I think we all deserve that. We do! *Everything* being love, happiness, wealth, great sex, attention, beauty, perfect kids, fun supportive friends, a hot body, and on and on. I don't want all the rest of these things that keep trying to tag along. I don't want to be told who I can and cannot be. I don't want someone who doesn't love me for me.

I remember an old story about the '80s band the Bangles. They had three or four lead singers, and that was always the way they performed. But then, the record company realized that Susanna Hoffs was a hot draw. She was petite and sexy, and they wanted to feature her more as the lead. So, they pushed the Bangles to use her as the lead singer. It messed up their groove. The band didn't last. The story didn't say so, but now I think that maybe it was because they were being forced to be something that they weren't. That just doesn't breed happiness in the long run.

Of course, that leads me to the question: Am I loving him for who he truly is? I don't think I am. It's all part of who he is, the way he's faking it. Maybe I need to be able to laugh it off. I'll do what I want and tell everyone, *Oh yes, that's just Pete! He likes to define people by his own standards, and he likes to project an image. That's just Pete!*

No, there's something different about that. That's too much on other people. Then we can say, *Yes, that's Veronica, she reads about witches and is fascinated by pagan philosophy. That's just her!*

There. Nothing to do with anyone else at all. I think.

But lots of people might see it differently. It could be construed that my liking things affects my husband and my daughter. Is that possible? Do they? And wouldn't it be OK even if they did?

I get up and go look in the hallway mirror. There I am. Wouldn't it be OK to be a witch, to believe what I see as truth and beauty? Wouldn't that have a positive effect on all involved, if I could share it with those close to me or at least have it shine though in my life, the way someone who's all "filled with God" would?

Sallow brown eyes stare back at me from not enough sleep. My hair has a teensy shine to it. When curly hair manages to get greasy, you know it's nasty. I turn to the side and assess what I see. Everything is relatively in its place. Except my tits. They've turned into pancakes since breastfeeding. Sand dollar pancakes. This bra isn't helping.

I shuffle away and hear Annie stirring on the monitor.

Annie's in bed, tucked in for the night. I have fixed a vodka martini, and it is warming me inside already. Of course, it's about seventy degrees outside, but whatever. I'm pretending.

The sun has set, and lights are turning on in neighboring houses. People are heading home from after-dinner walks with their kids, and I find myself again gazing out the window pensively. It's pretty like this, suburbia. There's a warmth to it right now, something likable about it. Even the sight of a minivan pulling into a nearby garage can't diminish this just-past-magic-hour feeling.

I like when you look at a house at night, the lights all on inside, and sometimes people are bustling about inside. It's like the flicker of a candle from inside a paper lantern. Line them all up, and it's a beautiful row, creating a mellow, sweet ambiance. I'll go for a walk. Wait. I can't. Annie's here. Duh, V!

It occurs to me that this evening might be the perfect opportunity to conduct a bit of research on spells and the like.

I figure I could use one of those spells—one of the free ones, anyway. I need something in my life to be stirred up, because things are beginning to develop a stagnant odor. Sure, it is great to raise a child here and provide a stable environment, but isn't there more to life than this? I feel like I might either go crazy or shut down, one or the other, if I let this go on for too long. I feel like something has to change. No more dull stale acceptance. The what-if's are alive within me, and I can feel them coming out of their dormancy. They want to try, to change, to grow.

The stirring I feel is both old and new. I've never truly entertained these urges before. I wonder why not? And why now? Is it this new life I have put into the earth? Is that what is pushing me? I just want something. *Something.* I don't know what. All I do know is that I feel like I have awoken in some way. I can't go back to sleep, as nice as that would be. I just can't.

OK. I may not have all the answers, obviously. Yet I have established today some things that I want and don't want. I grab my laptop and sit on the sofa, martini half gone. I search. And search.

Finally, I have found a little thirteen-step guide to creating ritual magic[1]. I'll just have to make do with what I have right here. *It's mostly about intention anyway*, I figure. I copy it all down on a piece of paper and try to make a few notes. I am ready to get rolling.

---

1. Ann Moura, *Green Witchcraft*, Llewellen Publications (1996), p. 96.

1. Choose the timing of the spell.

Easy. Now. Now is my time of the spell. I am sure that they mean a cycling of the moon or something like that. Maybe I better check. I search. The moon is waxing, with the full one due in days. Good enough. Witches like things to be on the upswing. Or it seems like they should, anyway.

2. Outline the ritual and prepare the tools and materials.

Hmmm. Outline the ritual. Tools. Materials. I better get more serious. I move to the breakfast room table with the laptop and a notepad. This list of steps is kind of an outline of my ritual already. OK, so that's basically covered. Tools and materials. It looks like I am going to need some candles. Of course there are special ones for witch rites, but I've only got what I've got so it'll have to do. After some cabinet rummaging, I come up with several votives, a pink and a blue and a nice gold one from Yankee Candle. They smell great but it'll be smell overload with all of them lit. There should be a word for that. Over-smell. Like too many smells at once. Like cacophony is for sounds. Cacofumy?

I digress. I put them on a special plate that we got for our wedding. I usually reserve it for pies and things of that sort. I figure that could represent abundance and since we are broke most of the time and scraping by on our credit cards and living month to month, that can't be a bad thing.

So it looks like pink represents honor, morality, friendships, and emotional love, promotes romance and friendship, and is a standard color for rituals intended to bring affection. It's also a color of femininity. I wonder how they figured all that out? Blue means health and the Goddess (I like the sound of that one), water element, wisdom, light, inner harmony, peace. I need that one. Inner harmony? Delightful! Now for gold: the God, so I guess I have both sides covered there, success, mental growth, fast money or riches—*Oh, hells yeah on that, maybe a lottery win will be in my future*, then I scold myself for thinking that because, *This shouldn't be about greed, V, so quit it*, but you know how sometimes your mind goes off by itself and things just pop in there—and healing energy, intuition, divination, and fortune. That's a good one.

I see too that in these rituals they add a lot of essential oils to their candles. I doubt that the Yankee Candle scents of Sunflower and Blueberry Scone are exactly what they had in mind. I know I have some herbs around here. I had some basil that's still OK on the fridge. I pick off a few leaves and decorate my candle plate. There. I look it up. This site says it's good for both "banishing" and "money." Hmm. I wonder if that would mean I would be banishing my money? That sounds like a bad idea. I throw it away. I hope it isn't bad that it was touching my candles. There are lots of herbs and scents listed, one of which is Dragon's Blood. For real? Must just be a name. I need to get some of that though, just to exoticize my recipes. Anyway, I blow off herbs for today.

This witch stuff is complicated. At least there's the internet. But you have to be really in touch with the earth. I've got some work to do.

There is a step for taking refreshment, so I make sure to lay that out. One site recommends "Cake and Wine." I am down to check those boxes. I have a dark chocolate truffle and an open bottle of Cabernet that Pete was drinking a couple of days ago. Close enough. I pour a glass at the ready.

So that's enough tools and materials.

3. Purify yourself.

Huh. Purify myself. I showered tonight and washed that grease right out of my hair. I am clean in the physical sense. I am sure there are things I could purify but for now, I go into the kitchen and wash my hands. That's good. I feel clean and pure. Now I have that Outkast song in my head, *So Fresh and So Clean*. I wonder if that's pure.

Moving on.

4. Purify the working space.

OK. I decide on Natural Baby spray cleaner. I wipe everything down. Hope that counts. Although, maybe they mean like burning incense or sage or something? I don't think I've had incense since college. Maybe a match would work. I light a big fireplace match and wave it around. It smells good. I try to think about purification. I think about telling all bad energies, *out with you!*

5. Create a sacred circle.

I don't know what this one means. I point with my finger in a circle around myself, take a sip of martini that has gotten warm a tiny bit by now, and leave it at that.

6. Have an invocation.

All the ones I find online have been a little complicated and, well, dark for my taste. I decide to wing it. Because why break form now?

I put my computer and my martini out of the circle and get more serious about this.

I begin a prayer and invocation.

I close my eyes and wonder where to begin. I start talking.

"Oh Goddess, God, powers that listen and powers of nature and sky, please hear me tonight. I don't know you yet, but I want to. I ask for you to listen, and I ask for help. I honor the spirits all around us, all the time, and I honor nature, that natural, deep beauty that so often gets ignored through the bustle of daily life." I'm kind of impressed with myself. I keep going. "I hope here tonight to invoke you in my own life, to bring about all these things that a human needs, that a woman needs: love, peace, understanding, all those things. You know what I'm talking about, right? Less stress. More compassion. I feel like I *want* all the time, I *want* and I *don't want*, and you in your divine knowledge can lead my life in a path of whatever it is that I *need*, I don't want to be greedy, of course not, but at the same time I know whatever I'm doing isn't working. I need the real thing. I need me. I need myself, to be whatever it is I am and to love that." Something in me is surprised to hear myself say that. But I like it, and I know it's true. This feels really good, this asking. "I ask for guidance and strength and peace, throughout whatever comes my way, and the strength to be me, to be that person I need to be to be truly happy. Oh, and the wisdom and ability to get in tune with nature."

Now what?

Sheepishly, I add for the first time what they say in *The Craft*. "Blessed be."

OK. I like it. But I'm glad no one is listening. Next step.

7. Perform the ritual observance.

To me, this means lighting the candles. I figure I will talk out loud. I light each one with a different match, asking for whatever that candle represents. I go pink first. "I light this candle to bring friendship and support and emotional love. Especially, emotional love in my closest relationship." That's good. Simple. To the point.

Gold is next. I am saving blue for last since it represents the Goddess. That just screams important to me. I light the gold candle with my long, silly match, which is getting too large of a flame on it. I light the candle and say my thing while shaking it out. "I light this candle for intuition, mental growth, success, and," I feel it bubbling up and I can't resist, I just can't, so I add, "any fast riches that would like to befall me." I immediately worry. What if that means someone might die? "But not at the expense of anyone else, though. Pure and clean." There. I nod in agreement. "For my intuition to be clear and for me to pay attention to it."

Now, blue. I strike a new match. "I light this candle, my final candle of the ritual, for the Goddess," I pause, "and the goddess within myself. I light this candle to bring her out, that strong divinity. To bring about her wisdom, light, inner harmony, and peace." A little voice in the back of my mind whispers, yeah, *is that all*? I know it is a lot. But I am going to ask. It says online that it is important to actually imagine yourself doing the things you desire or just at least really imagining yourself having whatever it is you are asking for. Kind of like *The Secret*, only I'm not asking for a bike or a check in the mail. I mentally realize that while I was doing my envisioning, Pete was nowhere to be found. But here I ask, anyway, for all these things, with or without him, whatever that may mean. Nothing ventured, nothing gained.

"Blessed be."

Again, I am glad no one is listening.

8. Raise and direct the energy.
9. Earth (ground) the residual power.

I take these together. Like a little dance. I should probably study how to do all this; I will probably laugh at this feeble attempt one day when I am high in my castle like Stevie Nicks.

I think I am channeling the tai chi I have seen on TV. I pretend that there is a little ball of energy in front of me, and I raise it up. I direct it at the lit candles, at myself. I let it go inside the circle. I imagine it that way, anyway. I allow any residual power to fall to the tile, which I will pretend is the earth. I press my palms flat to the ground between (I feel like saying "betwixt") my feet. Nice.

10. Take some refreshment.

Truffle and wine time! I savor it in my imaginary circle. It's hard not to feel happy—and a little silly, I must admit. I embrace the happy energy and let it be all around this. That certainly can only help my little spell or prayer or whatever you want to call this thing I'm performing.

11. Acknowledge the Lady and Lord.

Um, now, this one sets me back a little. Whatever I was reading was really into this Lady and Lord thing and I didn't really get into that idea. Plus, I haven't done anything really right yet, so why start now? I prefer to think of the "God" and "Goddess" anyway. Lady and Lord? What would that even be? I looked it up earlier and it was akin to the God and Goddess, so to me, this harkens to the male and female within us all and in nature, so I use that. I figure, rather than say something I read online and not know what the hell I am talking about, it's probably more effective to find some way of saying something that has some meaning to me, something real that I can put my heart into. Even if some of what I believe comes from a movie about four high school witches.

I take a deep breath. "I thank you, God, Goddess, Male, Female, Yin, Yang, all that is within me and all that is a part of life force around us, thank you for listening and aiding me throughout this ritual. I ask these things with a sincere heart and want them solely for the purpose of bettering not only my life and my child's life and the lives around me, but also to make the world a better place by being in harmony with my true nature and light." I am a little surprised at what is flowing right out of my mouth. "Thank you for your guidance. I ask that I be kept aware of anything that you want to show me."

I then envision a light being held within me. I add something I read online that I really liked. "I came in love, and I depart in love."

I consult my list.

12. Release the elementals.

I go around clockwise and point to four different points in front of me. "Earth, we are one, please depart in peace as we stay one." I proceed to same something close to the same for the Air, Fire, and Water. I feel very Craft-y with this step.

13. Open the circle.

I close my eyes and envision light being drawn into me, which is something I read online; they like the light to be blue, and that's my favorite color, so I stick with blue.

I peep my right eye open to read what to say next. I press my palms to the third eye area of my forehead. I have never exactly known where that is supposed to be but I just go with that spot between my eyes. "The circle is open yet the circle remains as its magical power is drawn into me." I read something like that online, too.

I hold that for what seems like a few minutes. It felt like it should be significant.

The instructions then said to let the candles burn for an hour. I like how the sun has gone down; it is providing dim, warm light. I get up and turn off the living room lamp and just sit, staring at the candles. I feel a little glow within me. A pilot light of change, lit.

I feel a little dazed and a little excited, all at the same time, like I have just passed some milestone. I was so excited and ready to get going on this that it has all been like following a recipe that you only read the ingredients for, then just dive right in and realize halfway through that you don't have a Dutch oven or really even know what that is but you just hope it's a big pot and fly by the seat of your pants.

I sit, staring—at the candles, out the window, at the glowing windows of the too-closely situated neighbors.

I remember a time when I was sixteen. I think back to that day. It was Mother's Day 1989, and my parents had forbidden me to date this guy, Cash, because he smoked pot, among other disreputable things they had heard. Of course,

I dated him anyway. Cash and I got along really well, so we kept it up. Plus I liked his name. *Cash*. It made him seem very cool to me.

That day I had sneaked over to his place by telling my parents that I was going out with a friend on her family's boat. Instead I have a distinct recollection of showing Cash my new panties from Victoria's Secret. We had been making out and talking and doing whatever in his room, and I was standing up and saw my dad walk through the yard, past Cash's bedroom window, around to the side of the house, and into the garage. Panic filled me. All I could think was, *Oh, shit.* Over and over. *Oh shit. Oh shit.*

I knew we had to walk outside so I just shifted into zombie mode. I shut down and walked out there with Cash. My dad could instill the fear of God in anyone; he was six feet four and could put on a deep voice that boomed and bellowed and shook your ribcage. I saw it coming. The words were short and terse, and his top lip curled under as he spoke. His head moved a little like a bobble head doll as he ordered me to drive home. I have no idea if he said anything to Cash; I can't remember. What I do remember in vivid detail is that I arrived home after a drive full of all possibilities of thought—things like, *Well, I have a gas card. How far could I get without them tracking me after my last fill up? Could I make it to Los Angeles and pull a Tracy Lords?*—but like a machine, my arms and legs controlled the car right home to my house, the same split-level, off-white brick structure that had been part of my life since I was two days old.

I got there, went inside, and sat on a chair in the den, staring out the window. My parents went somewhere. They told me they were leaving—probably to talk about just what the hell to do with me, because I was such a little rebellious liar. Of course, I blamed them completely and still kinda do, because I always thought that they put too many restrictions on me. It was like a vicious cycle. They would say they didn't trust me and put more restrictions on me; I would then lie to get to do whatever I wanted because I thought the restrictions were excessive.

So there I sat, in that chair, staring, and then they were home. Just like that. It turned out that they were gone for about two hours, but I sat still and stared the whole time. They then thought I was on drugs, of course—drugs Cash had forced upon me. But I had learned that telling them anything just got me in worse trouble usually so I kept my mouth shut. They asked me, "Have you been sitting here the whole time we were gone?" I remember saying yes. They were convinced that there was LSD use or something really horrific to their '50s-bred sensibilities.

I felt a little out of it, even though that day, I had ingested absolutely no substances. I was just out of it for those hours. I had been in some weird zone, a zone where I felt like something had shifted, like I didn't care anymore. They decided to have me drug tested. Postscript, I came out negative after smoking pot only five days before. This was in the days before the cleanse things that you could buy, too. Not sure how I came out negative, but I sure did thank my lucky stars for that one. They would have sent me to rehab in no time flat, no doubt. That was hot in my high school, people going to rehab for tiny amounts of drugs.

I said a lot of internal *whews*, mopped my brow, and put on my indignant attitude. I gloated and said, "I told you so," and all that. They apologized. I was still in trouble for seeing Cash, and they put me on a short leash. Not that short though, I guess, because they never took away my car.

I feel a similar way to this right now, and I haven't since then. A little dazed and little stunned, all is quiet, and time could slip away from me, hours could go by, and I wouldn't be the wiser. I let them. I let time become completely relative and external and irrelevant. I sit. In peace. It felt like an internal shift had taken place, just like before, but a shift to what? I don't care right now. I just let it be. Everything just is.

 *Five*

WHERE THERE'S SMOKE, THERE'S FIRE.

I wake to the sound of sweet baby talk through the monitor the next morning. I feel good. My intense zone-out that was similar to the one from nearly two decades earlier felt like a meditation, like a rest, like my mind had just been taken out and put on a shelf for a little while, and that was nice. I like the idea of taking my brain out and leaving it for a while. It can't get the best of me that way. It can't search for those little troubling details that it so loves to find and belittle me with, over and over. It can so very easily find things to harass and torture me with, and it has gotten so good at it over the years. The respite, however brief, was greatly appreciated— especially when it could have beaten me up about being a heathen and how everyone would think I was going to hell.

I am not sure why that even matters. I get all bothered by the fact that others might think I would be going to hell when clearly I don't even believe in it at all. Silly. But when we are raised with that to keep us in line, with that fear to keep us on the straight and narrow, it sticks. It creeps into our psyches and sets up camp there. It likes to have a little home, a little spot to flourish, fear does. It gets all happy when it gets to have a say in things, thoughts, decisions. I wish I could pick it up and take it out, too, the way I pretended that I did my brain. Stupid fear. Why should it even matter what anyone else thinks when I feel like I am living my life right? I don't know. It just does. It just makes something seem more valid if someone believes it. Like one person can say, "I believe in hell," and another says, "I don't believe in it"; it somehow seems like when they believe, it becomes more real, more actual, as if its realness will grow out of belief. Could that be possible? God, I hope not.

I am going through the motions today. Get baby up, feed baby, play with baby, take walk with baby, feed baby snack, la la la and on and on and on. It is sweet, and she is sweet. But days can be long and monotonous with a baby. I feel a nag deep down, a little something that tells me things are going to change and I am going to be the one who changes them. But I kinda leave it there, leave it alone. It's faint, like a voice on the phone when you've dropped the receiver. When the days pass like this, it's too easy to be complacent. I don't even know what the life I really want looks like anymore. This is what it is. I do it and go through the day-to-day, but when I think about what I would change it to if I could? I don't have the answer.

I close my eyes for a moment and imagine. I push myself for a minute, push myself to imagine what I want life to look like. There's me, there's Annie. We are happy. I feel free. I feel different. It feels good. I see the city. I see a home we walk to. I feel the city not too far away. I feel people around, I feel a lifeblood energy. I want this. But I have no idea how to get there.

Two days pass like this. I live life the same as always, managing to barely pay bills but driving my base-model Lexus; shopping at the grocery store and charging what I don't have the cash for; consuming and mothering and all that. It's Tuesday night and my main connection to the outside world has been the fucking playground. I'm bored. I'm restless. I have vodka.

Xander is back in town from New York. "Come over," I tell him over the phone. "Come over, and I'll make you dinner. I have martinis. I have cigarettes."

Little girl's in bed and Xander shows up. Ever on time. We kiss on the lips, and I love it but feel just a tiny bit embarrassed, like I always do.

"So what's up?" he asks.

"I don't know. Yes I do. But I just don't want to say things out loud." I tend the trout that's sautéing. He can cook it better, and we both know it. "You sure you don't want to take over this concoction? You're so good at it!" I slyly give a sidelong glance to him to butter him up.

"I'll make a sauce at the end."

"Yes! I love your sauces." I scrunch my shoulders up as high as they'll go and close my eyes in anticipation. "Happiness is food these days. Isn't that sad?"

"No. At least I have that, since I'm not getting laid."

"I don't understand that! What about in New York? There's tons of hot guys!"

"I'm just working too much! Besides, I'd probably meet some twenty-year-old and just hook up for a day or night . . ." His voice trails.

"And why would that be bad? Hello?" I frown and stare, and we both laugh.

"I know. I just need to find someone here. You still need to help me set up my Match.com stuff. I need more pictures on it, like in different settings so it looks like I'm doing different things."

"Like a photo shoot? Fine! We'll take some tonight! I can set up a little studio in the garage." I poke the trout and check the cauliflower in the oven. "And hey, how was New York? We haven't even discussed that."

He glosses over his fabulous life. "We had to bring up some jewelry for a shoot. It was Christina Aguilera on *Vanity Fair*."

"Wow! Was it Annie Leibowitz?"

"Yeah, but we didn't get to see any of that. We just took that big tanzanite necklace, and Andrew is bringing it back on Friday."

"Dude, I'm all over that Annie Leibowitz for your match profile. I'm gonna channel her." I open a bag of salad without it exploding. Little victories. "That's a big cover, though. Congrats."

"Yeah. But I'm sure she'll look like some kind of drag queen. Why does that one always look like she's in costume?"

"Because she is. Maybe we all are. I don't care though. I always feel like kicking some ass when I listen to her music." I crouch down a little bit, into a kung fu pose, and incorporate some arm action. "Like I'm this kick-ass bitch who doesn't take shit from anybody and lives life on her terms and fuck 'em all!"

He chuckles, and I do, too. "Wait a minute," he says. "So why is food your only happiness?"

My mood falls a little bit. I pick up my martini and perch up on the counter directly across from him, at the little spot between the breakfast room and the kitchen. The speckled granite feels cold, even through denim. My Ugg-booted feet dangle down unattractively and look larger than they really are, and I slightly avoid his stare.

"What's up?" he persists.

"Something's wrong."

"Like, something right now?"

"No!" That makes me smile. "No. Or, yeah. Something's wrong with, like, my life. Something is . . ." I set my martini on the ledge next to me that overlooks the breakfast room and do a hand motion that looks like I am rolling a very large invisible spool. His handsome face and heavy lidded eyes stare back, patient, waiting like this wonderful friend always does, for the revelation he is half-expecting. I scratch my head and pick my drink back up. I keep making faces, stretching my lips out, or giving a frown, now that I can since my Botox has worn off, or biting my lower lip. "Something's not right here. I'm not happy, or not living my life the way I need to, or not feeling like Pete really even pays attention to who I really am, or something like that." The seeds of dissatisfaction have begun to sprout. I do know that it has begun to really grow, and I am watering them, right here, right now, with this conversation, good or bad.

"Do you not want to be with him anymore?"

"I don't know." The timer goes off. I hop down, cross to the oven, and shut it off, dealing with dinner on autopilot. I set the food back aside and look at him. "I don't have any idea what I want but I am just feeling like this isn't it, you know? It's so much easier sometimes to figure out what you don't want. Why is that?"

"Good question. We probably feel like there is something better out there for us so it's easier to say what we don't want than to be content with what we have. Not that I'm saying you should be, not at all, believe me. I am all for seizing the power to change what we can in our lives to make it more real. And that's what I've always loved about you. You work to make things real. You're a real person."

I tilt my head to the side and give a little smile. "Thanks. I don't feel all that real at the moment, though, but it's sweet of you to say." I press on my face with my hands. I press around my forehead and my temples and every tendon I can find in my face. I am sure that's a weird-looking little habit, but I hold way too much tension in my face so I constantly do it.

"Make this sauce. I'll do fresh drinks."

"K."

We sit and eat and drop the subject for a few minutes, but it inevitably comes back up. I tell him about Halloween, how stupid that all was, and I tell him about getting "caught" on the computer looking up witch stuff. He's interested, having been raised Catholic but not at all into it, and he doesn't give a shit what I do and lets me be. I love it. I am so very thankful for that.

"It sounds like you're figuring out who you really want to be," he says, "and that's good. People go for years without doing that. Sometimes their whole lives! Trust me, I've seen it."

"Yeah. I can't even get a handle on what's pushing me to proceed. But I can't seem to stop. I guess it's just, like, been in there, and some part of me thought everything would just be done for me. Does that make sense? Including this." I pause and let out an *ugh*-sound and massage my forehead a little. "But I want someone who loves me for the person I am, whoever that person is, that person that I figure out I want to be." I shove a huge salad bite into my mouth. There's probably something subconscious deep inside me telling me to shut up.

"I love you for that person."

I smile through the chewing. Very cute, I'm sure.

He goes on. "Don't we all, though? Shit. That's the million-dollar desire. That's the thing. Don't you feel like Pete loves you for exactly who you are?"

I make a pursed lip face and swallow, giving him a look.

"I guess that's a no." He laughs.

"It's a 'not even.' Look at what I just told you about the other night!" I calm down a little bit, taking a sip of my drink and a deep breath. "I'm not sure that he has ever loved me like that. Sometimes I wonder how many people get married because of timing, you know? Like, right place, right time, I'm in my twenties, everyone's doing it."

"God, I'm glad I'm not straight."

"Ugh. I wish you were."

We have a moment where we smile and look in each other's eyes. So sweet. We both laugh a little.

"He loves this *idea* of me. He loves this thing about fitting into society, or fitting into his family and mine. Or being what you are 'supposed' to be. Whatever that is." I slump over into a defeated posture.

"Everybody gets caught up in that, to a certain extent. But you have to remember that no one can tell you what you are supposed to be, and you are the one who has to live it. I think those facades can only make you happy for a little while. When you get real with it, when you lay there in bed at night and your mind is just going round and round, it all catches up and you have to be honest about things. You are the one who has to live with you, ultimately."

"Some people don't seem to do that. Like Pete."

"Right. All what I just said is true, unless you're a Republican and you don't think at all."

We both laugh at that. I am definitely glad that I am eating because I feel that martini. We leave the dishes and head outside with the pooches for a cigarette after dinner. It's good. Pete hates it when I smoke. But I have been doing it for too long, and sometimes I just want one. Or five. Like tonight.

"What's for dessert?"

I am sitting on the sofa, drunk. Probably not a good mother for being like this. I certainly couldn't drive anywhere if I needed to. Oh well, I shrug. I have lots of neighbors. Xander drove home but probably shouldn't have. We watched HGTV, we laughed, and I needed it, a friend to tell things to, that friend who always listens and always understands and always is willing to have a drink right there with you. And a smoke, too. Pete comes home tomorrow. Ugh. I like the peace around here when I have the entire place to myself. When things are mostly right where I left them, when life is simpler without a stupid husband mucking things up. I walk—or what passes for walking—over to the kitchen and add what's in the shaker to my glass. I know I shouldn't but when there's no one there to stop me, who cares. I plop back down onto the sofa and mindlessly stare at the TV. Is this happiness? Is this life? Alcohol takes me up and smacks me back down, hard. Usually I feel it the next day, but I think when my mood is already predisposed to negativity before drinking, it goes back there a lot more quickly.

I wish I could magically just cast a spell and fix everything. Doesn't it work like that? And what would I even change it *to*?

I wish I could just command power and make things happen. But I suspect it doesn't work like that. OK . . . I *know* it doesn't work like that. If there were really, truly, an easy way out of things, that would just be so nice. So *easy*. Or maybe it does work like that and I just *don't know how*. What if it does and I just haven't tried? I wish it would all be easy, I wish Pete would just die or drop off the face of the earth, and I know that I am an absolutely terrible person for thinking those things but I can't help it, there they are right there and fuck it, then I would have life insurance from him and I take another sip and all my problems would be solved I am sure and life would be magical anyway. Sober me is somewhere in there, too, and hears what's going on in my head and knows I am just getting it out, but she scolds me a little. I know. We have all these little people in there knocking around and this one, this negative bitch, is out right now.

I know that I should go to bed but instead I just keep staying up, flipping channels and drinking and going outside for a lonely smoke with the dogs every now and then. I stink like booze and cigarettes and don't care and should go to bed.

What am I going to do? That thought leads me into things I have never thought before, things that I can't imagine even though they are things people do every day. It's funny that I can think, *I wish he would die in a car accident,* and not mean it but then not even be able to think the big D word. I have never entertained that thought. Maybe it is because I knew if I did, it would really be a possibility. Maybe too many couples make that mistake of not letting it be a possibility instead of paying more fucking attention so it doesn't happen.

I make the big leap and head for bed. I know I am getting too drunk and I have to be able to wake up from the baby monitor. I stare at it and know that the morning is going to come all too soon, and the day will be here before me, slapping me into reality, forcing me to face the light and the sun, literally and figuratively. I will squint and my head will throb, but I will not regret this episode—I will not regret the thoughts I have. I hope that they are leading me to wherever it is and whoever it is that I need to be. I am not making sense anymore and I am such a bitch and I crawl into the bed on Pete's side because I like it better than mine and I close my eyes and the racing of my mind is quieted and I am thankful for that and I drift, drift.

 *Six*

THERE'S A STORM AT THE DOOR.

Day breaks and I wake before my toddler alarm clock. Always a drinking hazard of mine—I can't sleep in after too much to drink. I look at the clock though bleary eyes and focus on the numbers, trying to make sense out of them. 8:28. The numbers of my birthdate. Oh, god. Why hasn't Annie woken up yet? My mind immediately thinks the worst, and I start to freak myself out. *She's dead.* God. I am sick with fear. This isn't the first time this has happened, so I know that most likely she is fine, but the depressants that I ingested last night make me think the worst immediately. I grab the monitor and turn the volume all the way up, pressing my ear against the speaker. I hold my breath. I hear breathing on the other end. Thank God. Thank you, God, Goddess, Baby, whatever, *whew*. I snap right back to reality and head in to make some coffee. Because that's what I need to ingest. More substances.

I make a pot, and the first cup goes down fast and good. I pour a second, and Annie starts to stir. Mom-mode kicks in. I am feeling up to it. I start the motions, the boring, dull motions of daily life in the suburbs taking care of a child. At least there is the child, and that's the bright spot. But the irony of a child is that when you are with her, you want a break, want to get away and have a moment of peace for yourself, and when you are apart from her, you just want to be with her. Annoying. Makes you want to be more present but sometimes it just doesn't work.

I catch a glimpse of myself in the mirror. My hair has a mind of its own, but today it has a mind like mine—wild. It's piled atop my head in a bun, but half of it has come down. I am sure that I reek as well. This is one of those days when the first tooth brushing was just the ice breaker. Now I have added the scent of coffee to my breath. Thank God toddlers don't give a shit.

My day goes without incident. Pete calls once his phone is within range. He didn't shoot anything, no deer killed by him. Good. I can't take another dead deer head in my house. I know that he gets home today. I am not really looking forward to it, but I know that it is inevitable. Annie doesn't really know the difference at all just yet. She loves me, loves him, but I think we could simply be interchanged with about anyone else who treated her sweetly and she'd adjust within a week.

I decide to clean. I think sometimes, and especially today, it is some kind of metaphor for my soul, or for my life. Like, if I can make everything clean, scrub it down, it will all sparkle and shine through and be true and right and perfect. I get crazy. Annie is perfectly content to play with little toys, watch her sweet little shows, or play with her little table she can stand up and push buttons on. I furiously vacuum and dust and use products that I am sure are contaminating the environment but smell so lemony fresh and clean that I have a hard time resisting them. I mop the tile and move Annie from room to room, upstairs and downstairs. It keeps it interesting enough for her to think that something is happening. I clean like my life depends on it, I drink coffee, and I juice myself up further and get faster and more furious. It's fun. The Virgo girl inside me is partying hard now.

The inevitable arrival of Pete lingers as the day wears on. Annie naps her second nap of the day, and I decide to actually clean myself in my sparkling bathroom. I love being somewhere clean, especially when I feel good inside. It helps today, too, when I don't feel so good inside. All the coffee coupled with the substances from the night before have me jittery and crazy and not myself at all. It's a weird shower, and I suppose that it probably wasn't such a good idea for me to huff all those cleaning product fumes on top of everything else.

I feel like I just don't know if I can keep my mouth shut. Maybe that's a good thing, though. I suppose most people feeling like I do would open their mouths and spit it out, get it out, tell that person they are living with, the one who is supposed to love them fiercely and without limits. This is supposed to be a relationship like that; for god's sake, it's 2019, not 1959. We should be equal to our partners and feel comfortable telling them anything. Maybe I can do that. Maybe I can just sit down with him and say, "Hey. I'm feeling stifled. I'm feeling like you don't love me for who I am."

Maybe I can just stand up for myself and say exactly what it is that I want out of this whole relationship. And maybe he will listen. Maybe he will give me a big hug, maybe he will envelop me in his arms, maybe he will tell me that it's fine, as long as we are together, he doesn't care, it's all OK, and whoever or whatever I want to be, that's just all right.

I half-laugh at myself for fantasizing this way. I think this is such a long shot. After the very small discussion (if you could call it that) the other night about "not teaching our daughter that," I feel like this fantasy is insanely far-fetched. But I probably have to try. Can a marriage fall apart over something like this? What all can marriages fall apart from? Does there have to be an infidelity? Maybe this is like an infidelity. Maybe it's a dishonesty that is inherently like an infidelity; maybe if I started to secretly read up on spells, it would be like hiding an affair, hiding something that I didn't want him to know about. It sure would be nice to do it out in the open.

Sweet Annie is napping when I hear the deep mechanical burst of the garage door opening. A sick feeling falls in the pit of my stomach. I still look pretty shitty, even after the shower, but don't really care. I am just finishing up the whole cleaning frenzy I was on with some mopping. The house is sparkling. It makes me feel like internally, I am cleansed. There is something communion-like, something akin to forgiveness in having things this clean and tidy and orderly. They do say that cleanliness is next to godliness. That could be why. I wait. He doesn't come in. I wait some more. Finally, I tread lightly across the tile, wet spots reducing to the sides of each tile and shrinking by the second as they dry up and dull the sparkle. I peep out the door and see him, rustling through his big blue four-door monstrosity of a truck, pulling out guns and stuff and more stuff. I catch a glimpse of him and gear up to speak.

"Hi! How was it?"

He pokes his head up so he can see me through the driver's side window and the windshield, since I am still standing in the garage. "Hey!" he replies. "It was great! Mike got a buck."

"Can I help you?"

"Sure. Can you carry this?"

I cross through the garage and out to the driveway. He hands me a brown leather gun case that belonged to my father, and we quickly peck hello on the lips. I see his shirt then for the first time. I am semi-disgusted. It's a green tee with three boxes of drawings on it, like rest-stop-type drawings for bathrooms or something of the like. Underneath each box is a caption stating what the box contains a drawing of. First one: guns. Second one: God. It's represented by a cross. Because of course, there's only one God, and *he* involved a cross. Third one: country. This one has a flag in it. I ask myself: *This* is the person I am supposed to be able to talk with? To open up to about the fact that I want to be able to read about witches? I think that is more what our country should stand for, but something tells me that I would not get agreement with that at all.

"New shirt, huh."

"Yeah. We saw them last night when we went out to eat at the little store in town. I think everybody bought one. We thought they were kind of funny."

"Who all was there?"

"Well, Mike, of course, and both of his brothers came by at one point or another, and Drew, Joe, Vontour, Brady, and then Court, but Court only came for one night."

I bite my tongue about the shirt. Amazing to be able to find a group of seven or more people who all love that fucking shirt. I have hopes that I can make it disappear or "accidentally" spill bleach across it.

I start to lug the gun inside.

"Babe, leave it out, I need to clean it before I put it up."

"OK." I remember my dad cleaning his guns, the smell of WD-40 surrounding him. I actually loved that smell. It was one of the few times that my father was a captive—not really audience—but captive for conversation. I'd sit on the bear rug downstairs as he cleaned his guns when he returned from a hunting trip. He had a big gun case that he kept locked, not that I ever would have cared to get in there. The one gun that was actually dangerous to me and my friends wasn't kept under lock and key at all. No, it was simply kept tucked in the back of my father's nightstand drawer, tucked so far back that he was, I am sure, certain that I would never encounter it there, but kids go through everything and kids know where everything is. There's no hiding anything from a kid. My best friend growing up found pot in one of her dad's many shoe boxes. Shoe boxes are not as good a hiding place as you would think, apparently—even though I have totally hidden diet pills in my own shoe boxes before. I didn't want the questions from Pete. But back to the point. My dad's little loaded handgun was right within my reach, right where a child who isn't so prudent might pick it up and have an accident. I never mentioned it to my brother. I don't know if he

knew about it or not. He's a pretty nosy type, though. I bet
he knew. But why my mother allowed that to be within reach
of her children, I do not know. What if I had told a friend?
What if they had then begged to see it and picked it up? And
who knows what then?

Anyway, I tote the gun case into the bedroom and set it
down. Annie is stirring and probably needs a new diaper and
all the rest of it. I go to my little, tiny buffer, the one thing
that changes all conversations, the one we can't fight around.
(Even though we do sometimes.) She is the one thing that I
can absorb myself in when I want to check out of a conversation. She is the perfect way out when you need it—that's one
thing I will say about having a kid. Of course, there are those
times that you really want to stay or really want to finish that
conversation. It works that direction, too.

I get Annie and tell her that Daddy is home. We do all
those baby things we do, and I look in the mirror in her room.
I suppose that I could have made a little effort here since I
hadn't seen Pete in days. I guess I just didn't care that much. At
least, Annie looks cute. I look like some tired dog, still jittering
from too much vodka, nicotine, and caffeine. I have scrubbed
my mouth about five times today in hopes that the evidence
is erased. I don't feel like catching shit for smoking, not from
Mr. God, Guns, and Country. I take comfort in the fact that
I am sure I reek of coffee and it overwhelms all the rest of it.

We head down to the kitchen. All of Pete's things have
been dragged in and scattered around my nice clean house. I
attempt to cast a Zen spell of some sort around me. Like, I can
imagine a Zen light of blue surrounding my whole person. It
makes me immune to the disregard of the clean house.

He comes out of the master bedroom. "House looks great!" This makes me smile. I cock my head to one side. "Thanks for noticing." And that's all it took to soften me a bit.

We go through the motions. He does all his stuff he needs to do: swishing around, putting things away, showering, checking his email in his office. I do all the things I need to do: playing with Annie, feeding her dinner, bathing her, all the rest of it. Pete flits in and out, saying hi and talking sweet to her, spending a moment here, a moment there. The day passes uneventfully. I find the resolve to speak my mind fading. I would just rather keep the peace for now. Everything is normal, everything is fine, everything is quiet, and everyone is peaceful. I just want to coast on this.

Night comes, and everyone is in bed. I am tired from the night before and getting up so early. I want to sleep, and Pete wants to watch TV. He turns on the AppleTV, and I go to bed. No sex—not that I want it. I would rather quietly masturbate than do it with him right now. It's a lot less work. So I do, and I vaguely think and fall asleep instantly right after.

The next day dawns and is lovely. It's hard to believe that it is November, what with the seventy-degree weather and all. We dress in short sleeves. Pete is lazy, reading the paper and meandering to his office when the mood strikes. I am up, I am dressed, I have already done chores and laundry and bitterly unloaded the dishwasher, a task I loathe but am forced to do on a daily recurring basis with no outside help. Annie and I went to the gym and have made it back already to find

Pete ready to head to the gym. Oh well. Fine by me, see ya! I feed her lunch and go through those motions, that routine—always creatures of routine, she and I. I clean up Pete's wake and get her down for a nap. It's my time to relax now.

I sit at my laptop and decide to look up witch stores in Austin. I really dream of a safe space where no one will recognize me yet there will be some magic easygoing woman there who knows precisely what I need—who can save me from the hard work, tell me, "Oh honey, take this crystal, recite these words, and all your problems are solved." Can I conjure *her* ass up? I do like the searching, though. There's a beauty in the process that I really need to embrace. It's just like motherhood. It's easy to wish it to be at another juncture when we should appreciate the moment with that child because it will never ever come again.

What should I google? "Witch supply store Austin"? "Witch shop"? I start having some luck when I hear the garage door. I love how loud that damn thing is. Annie is used to it, considering that she has listened to it since birth practically, and it always gives me fair warning to wrap up anything I am doing that I don't want to be seen. It's so sad that I am even admitting that to myself. I hide the digital Post-it note that has the addresses of the shops on it and close up the computer.

Pete comes in and says hi and heads for the shower. About ten minutes pass, and the doorbell rings. I can see straight through the beveled glass. The guy on the other side looks Picasso-esque with his face and body caught through each glass piece and refracted to me. The sun is shining out there, and it's a beautiful day. I open the door and tilt my head a bit, to show that I have no idea what this is about. The dogs have been sufficiently shushed and get a look at the bottom of my shoe, shoving them back and back again until they give up; they know it's fruitless. I squint as the sun shines behind him, and I then get a good look.

He is a little disheveled. Something is off about this guy. It's like he tried to look presentable and acceptable, he tried to put on something he thought would look good to people in a suburban neighborhood, with his cheap blue plaid collared button-down and khaki pants with pleats, but the pants are slightly soiled and there is a smell of desperation wafting from him. He hasn't showered or shaved today—at least, I would be very surprised if he had—and his hair has that standing up dirty blondness to it, that unclean, greasy look that can be sexy on the right man. But not here. His teeth have seen better days. There is a chip on one of the front ones, and the stains from cigarettes indicate smoking from a young age. This guy can't be more than twenty-two. I look for a car, a vehicle of some sort, maybe something that has a carpet cleaning business name on the side or something, anything. Sometimes we get the people canvassing for clean water action and they don't have cars with them and that's OK and all. But this guy? No car. No other people. No clipboard, no paperwork.

My intuition says that something else is going on here. I am protective of the inside of my house and of myself. Not that I look like much; I was feeling skinny today because of the drinking and the coffee from yesterday and the days before, and I haven't changed and am still in my workout clothes.

"Yeah . . . can I help you?" I venture with trepidation. I do like to give people the benefit of the doubt. It is two o'clock on a bright and sunny day—not exactly the ideal time for illicit activities. Unless he thinks that all the men-folk are off at work.

"Hi, ma'am, how are you today." He continues without waiting for a response. "My name is Daniel, and I live over on Snapdragon. My father is Dr. Phillips, you know him, works over at Seton hospital. I am getting donations for our Bowie high school trip since we are going to Europe and we are needing sponsors for each of us to go." He pulls out a piece of paper from his back pocket, folded in eighths, and begins to unfold it.

This guy does not look like he is in high school. But whatever, I can't ever tell. Of course, I have no idea who this doctor he is talking about is, or if he even exists.

He continues. "This is information about our trip. We are going for three months with our class and need donations to help sponsor us."

I haven't said a word and I try to get one in. I start to ask a question but he rolls right past me.

"We have nineteen people going. It is a trip over the holidays to tour through Europe. We need to pay for the airfare and hotels and food. It is for my class through Bowie High. My father, Dr. Phillips, is right over there on Snapdragon, and we are hoping to get some donations from people in the neighborhood."

This guy is a crackhead.

He hands me the handwritten piece of paper. He continues to talk and say the same things, over and over, filling the space with his prepared speech and sometimes adding little things about the group or the trip or sometimes even bragging about himself. "The group has over 3.8 GPA. We all have GPA at the top of our class." I laugh inside that he threw that one in. I look down at the paper he has given me. It says Bowie High School, scrawled across the top and underlined twice. Then it has several lines of writing, most of which he has already covered with me. It has his name, Daniel Phillips, or what he says his name is anyway, and underneath that, "Class Trip to Europe," and then it has some dates around Christmastime. It's about as generic as it gets. I especially like that it just says "Europe trip."

I find a way to get a word in. "Where in Europe will you be going?"

"Um, ma'am, it's a trip to Europe, to Paris and to Germany, to learn about history in those countries." He is speaking rapidly and seems a little annoyed that I asked a question. I hear Pete stepping up behind me. Oh boy. He won't like this at all.

"Hey." Pete steps into the conversation.

"Hey. This is Daniel, and he says he is raising money for a Bowie trip to Europe."

Daniel stands his ground. He starts in on the speech, this time to Pete. Pete is angry and mistrustful immediately, and not nearly as nice as I am. I was letting this guy talk for a moment, and then I was going to turn him away somehow and wish him luck. I didn't want to call his bluff but was just focusing on getting the door between him and me.

But Pete is angry.

"You need to just go on. Get out of here."

I can't imagine that angering this guy is a good way to go. But men have to do their whole testosterone thing, I guess.

Daniel interjects that he was just trying to collect donations for his trip, and he throws in another bit about his father, the impressive doctor, living over on Snapdragon.

Pete gets terse and condescending. "You know what, that's all good and fine, but you need to leave our house right now and go do this somewhere else, OK? You probably need to take it to a different street. Just keep it moving out of here, OK?" The pointing finger is out. He speaks slowly and deeply, nodding while he's talking, that old waiter and waitress technique of getting people to agree with you when they want you to order dessert; his voice rang low, too, putting on that masculine deep intonation that is probably a part of nature's intimidation factor.

We both pull the dogs back again while looking at Daniel.

I can tell that Daniel is pissed at the way he's being treated, but when you are that full of shit, it doesn't really matter. I lied to my parents for years with a practiced indignance. It must go with the territory of being an effectual liar—helps you keep up the façade. I suppose it can make it easier to spot, too, when you have actually done it.

We close the door behind Daniel. I look at Pete, wide-eyed and start to laugh. "Oh my god! Crazy guy!"

"What was that?" Pete doesn't look amused at all. I can understand that, I guess. He looks angry and confused.

"I don't know. He just rang the doorbell and started going on about his dad the doctor and his GPA and big trip to Europe." I chuckle and continue, "I was just like, oh my gosh, how do I get this guy to go away?"

"You can*not* answer the door when there's someone like that out there." Emphasis on *not*.

"Well, I didn't know until it was already open. Sorry, but he did end up going away."

Pete was getting madder, and I found it to be ridiculous and highly irritating. "No, V," I have heard this tone before, many times, "you need to *not* answer the door then."

"What? Not answer the door?"

"That could have been someone who wanted to come in and hurt you and Annie, or take Annie, rob us, anything, if I hadn't been here."

"It's the middle of the day, and that isn't what happened. Besides, it isn't like that happens every day."

"Yes, but remember when you bought those steaks?"

Oh, I knew that one was going to be thrown back in my face. One time, last year, some shady guy with a truck full of steaks had come around and for some reason I bought about ten expensive filets from him because I couldn't figure out how to make him go away. They were stupidly expensive and I knew I fucked up, but what the hell. At least it wasn't magazine subscriptions that never materialize. I don't tell Pete this, but once, in college, I got stung by that little gem of a scam, too. I sense that now would not be a good time to advertise failure with front-door opening. "Yes. I know. I made a mistake on that one. But I wasn't doing that this time. I was totally glad that you were here though."

"Ha! Yeah! Thank goodness I was here, V! You just can't answer the door."

He must be joking, I think with an internal laugh. "OK, you're not serious, right? You don't want me to answer the door? In the middle of the day?"

"You just can't. Not when it's not safe for you and Annie."

"What if it's a neighbor?"

"Then you just look through the glass and know who it is and then open the door."

"And if it's, you know, someone like canvassing for politics or something like that? What am I supposed to do then?" I am getting pissed at the ridiculous nature of this request. "I just peer through the glass to make out who it is and then tell them to go away through the door, that I can't open it?"

"Yeah!" he replies, nodding his head.

By this time, I have sidled over to my kitchen desk and am sitting in front of my computer, brow furrowed, knees together and staring at him hard. He is in the kitchen, pacing around like a tiger, probably still thinking about Daniel. Or, should I say, "Daniel."

"Yeah! That's right," he says. "That's gonna be what you have to do from now on. I do not want you opening that door for people."

I am stunned. Where is that man who used to make me laugh? Where is that guy who loved me and thought that I was at least a little bit able of taking care of myself? All this on the heels of him being gone for three days. This is ridiculous, and I am stopping it now. "No! I am not going to peep through the glass and be like, 'Sorry, but my husband won't let me open the door!' What do you think, that I'm an idiot?"

"Well, you opened the door for that guy!"

"So what! It's not like we live somewhere we need bars on the windows. This is a pretty good neighborhood. Plus, you know what? If someone wants to get us, then guess what, they're going to get us. They'll figure out a way if they want to." There is a pause. I go on. "And this is my house, too. If I want to answer the door in the middle of the day, then guess what," I say, full of attitude, feeling my neck move with each word I utter, "I'm going to."

"V," his voice is furious and loud now, and he speaks in what I believe would qualify as a yell. He would most likely call it something like speaking strongly, or something silly like that, but it qualifies. My defiance has further infuriated him. "You are not going to answer that door!" He points his right index finger directly at me and peers down it, blood rushing to his face, fury in his eyes. "And that is going to be a law in this house!"

Oh, no, he did not just make a law on me in *my* house. *Our* house. Or rather, I wish it was *our*; it seems more like *his*. I feel a calm wash over me. A single thought sits in my head, floating like a balloon, wanting to come out, to be made more of a reality by being passed through my lips and born into the world. The thought is important, and I want to say it, I really do. I want him to know how bad it is getting, and that this is so wrong for me—it might work with some girls, but not with me; the three-word thought just hangs there waiting, waiting for me to get honest and stand up for what is going on inside me. The thought sits. *You're losing me.*

You're losing me.

I know that I can't live with someone like this. You can, I think, love someone, but not at all want to be with them, not want to spend your life with them.

This conversation is over. I am shaking my head and I roll my chair away to face my desk in disgust. There isn't anything else to say. He isn't being rational, and this isn't a discussion. I review what just went down as I am poised over my laptop, fingers in place but still and not typing, my mind racing to grasp what he was telling me. I start to go through it all: the mental image of me peering through the glass to see if it is someone I know, and this person seeing me, in the middle of the day, a Jehovah's Witness staring back perplexed, perhaps, wondering to himself what is wrong with this woman, as I line my mouth up with the seam of the door to get through the words, "Sorry, I'm not allowed to open the door!"

I am just not going to live my life in fear like that. There is a lot to be said for prudence and caution, yes, but I still live in a nice neighborhood in the suburbs on a cul-de-sac. I'll be damned if I get a law put on me to not answer the door if I want to. He crossed a line with me. I have always been the type of person who can just be done with something or someone. A switch can get flipped when I am treated a certain way and pushed past a certain point—a switch that clams me up and turns me off. I feel like that now, like it is just done; I refuse to be told not to answer the door, and I refuse to feel censored about what I can and cannot teach my daughter. While these things are not a huge deal and I know that many people have it much worse off, I still refuse to live like this.

They say that there are circles of need that have to be met for a human. The first circle contains the basics, like food and shelter. Then the circles go out from there. Outer circles get into emotional needs. We have evolved to where we, in this country, anyway, mostly have the inner, more basic needs met and have moved on to needing those psychological and emotional needs met, too. When they are not, we seek them, thinking that we must meet them, because they can take on a greater importance when those other needs are already met.

I know that this is an outer circle, but I believe that it has to do with love. This is not how I see love working. I don't know if I am supposed to explain that to the one who claims to love me the most. Are you required to spell it out? Is that what counseling is all about? I don't want counseling. That sounds grueling. I don't want to explain. I want someone to innately understand that to love me, you have to give me room to be whoever I am and explore things and answer the fucking door. But maybe then give me fucking tips on staying safer. Just . . . *stop*.

I sit, still and quiet, but with a storm brewing inside.

 Seven

EMBRACE THE GODDESS WITHIN.

I think I might have shut down with this marriage. My heart isn't in it any more. Certainly, there's no getting laid for him or me. I don't care, and I don't want it anymore. OK, not entirely true. I just don't want it from him.

These thoughts coast with me up the three-lane highway that is Mopac Expressway. Annie is entertained in the backseat, holding her little zebra that is the flavor of the week and cooing baby words at it, between stares out the window and looks at Mama. She is such a good girl. I want so much for her. The desire for her to have whatever she wants, to get to be the person she wants to be, burns inside me. I wonder if that isn't what has spurred all of this on in some way. I know that as a woman, I have to set the right example for her; of course, in my mind, the "right" example is quite a subjective term. I look out at the greenbelt passing by, the trees still green mostly, the leaves not over-ripening with what should be the heart of the fall.

My focus shifts to the cars around me, all those people, and I wonder about them. Are they living how they want? What concessions do they make on a daily basis? Of course, this is Austin, a place that prides itself on being *weird*. That is evident wherever you go; you can find someone who is really living life on their terms, or at least it appears that way when you see some beautiful girl with two sleeves of tattoos down her arms. It's hard to tell a person like that what to do, isn't it? I have the flash of when Pete forbade me to get any more tattoos. I only have one, but through having it redone over the years, it has grown a little bit. Last time I indicated I was thinking about another one, he said flatly, "No more tattoos."

I remember the other day, when I wondered where that guy I had fallen in love with had gone, the one who had made me laugh, the one who I thought I had to marry, and the one I would always have so much fun with. But maybe a better question is, what happened to that girl? That girl who defied convention, got tattoos when her family would have freaked out (which they did, years later, when they found out). What happened to that girl who felt the way I do now? Where has she been, and why did it take getting here to bring her back?

Annie says something about the cars around us and a red truck. We talk for a moment, some baby talk about trucks and cars, and I define traffic for her. "I wike it," she says. And then I see that it has been her, it has taken this little person, this woman potential, this someday-to-be-standing-on-her-own-two-feet human being that has brought this out of me. Or should I say, brought this *back* out of me. In bringing a child into this world, it has reminded me of how I see things. Being right isn't about going to church or living by rules set out by other people. While, of course, I respect a moral code, it's more about "do unto others" and all that Golden Rule business rather than imposing a falsely right way of living. Live and let live, that's fine by me—and be kind. She has been the gentlest reminder of all to be who I want to be, and to me, that is the best example I could ever set for her. I hope that someday she can understand that. Because something in me, deep down, knows that life is not going to remain the way it is at this moment. It simply can't.

We turn onto South First Street after running a few errands. The main errand we are out for today has been the one I have been putting off, even though I am insanely curious and nervous and all those emotions that live right near each other in the little land of feelings.

I peer out at the addresses before me and get closer and closer. I see the numbers getting higher, I determine which side of the street it's on; I keep going and realize that this witch store is in a strip mall, of all things. I think that I was expecting something out of the movies, like something all mysterious and hidden by ivy (OK, cue *The Craft* again), something with curtains and a hand-painted sign and a little bit of darkness and ambiance.

But here it is, Ancient Mysteries, not looking the least bit ancient or mysterious. Instead, it looks modern and sedate. I take a deep breath and get out of the car, opening the back door and stalling a bit to get Annie out of her car seat. She's all happiness and light today. I take that as a good sign.

I decide to brave it. I am here, and I have to go in. This is about the least intimidating witch store I could ever imagine. It's next to a place called Kids & Cats, for heaven's sake!

I open the staid business door and semi-pretend it's an old door from a pagan church. That makes me laugh. Annie smiles up at me. We walk inside, Annie clinging to me like a baby koala. The retail floor is roughly seven hundred square feet, a measurement estimate I weirdly make in every store after having my own years ago (which was nine hundred, just so you know). It has glass shelves throughout the middle. The mix of scents from the numerous candles and essential oils surprisingly pleasant.

I think Annie likes it. She is all wide-eyed and perky and seems to want to know where we are. I tell her we are at a special crystal store and not to touch anything, and I avoid the mention of the word witch. She learns little words too quickly, and I am afraid she might repeat it. I guess though that the store considers itself, actually, a "metaphysical" supply store. I love that. I took a metaphysics class in college. I was the only female and was often too embarrassed to say anything, except for one time when we were having a discussion about a VW van, and our teacher was asking about whether or not it would be the same van if, over time, all the parts were replaced one by one from a company in Australia. It would look the same, but was it really the same van? I made the comparison then that our bodies do the same thing by sloughing and regenerating cells, so are we the same person? Of course, we are, if we believe we are. My sole comment of the semester went over well. I was relieved. So now, when I think metaphysics, that's what I think of. That incident alone. I can't even say what the word "metaphysics" even means anymore. What a pathetic excuse for a philosophy major I am.

I start to look around. There is a library directly to my left, consisting of two particle-board imitation cherry wood five-shelf bookcases, with titles that run the gamut of metaphysics to witchcraft, but it still doesn't look too comprehensive. I keep Annie on my hip as I flip through a few, one titled, *Everyday Witch A to Z: An Amusing, Inspiring & Informative Guide to the Wonderful World of Witchcraft*. I like it. I wish I could buy a book, but short of stashing it in someone else's house, I really have no idea where I would ever put it and not get busted. Other titles pique my interest, like *Wicca: A Guide for the Solitary Practitioner*, and *Great Goddesses*. I smile and move on, the back of my mind churning with ideas on where I could possibly hide that contraband.

I would love to create an altar. That's what's sneaking around inside me. But I am afraid. I am afraid of being chastised by my husband—as a sinner, as a worshipper of false idols. Whatever that means. I don't want to worship anything. I want to live in harmony and peace and let my heart be free. This thought makes a little lump rise in my throat. I don't want to live scared. I want to live happy. That's all it is.

I had read about the importance of crystals. That is really why I have come. There are literally crystals everywhere, with cards next to them that say what they're good for. Selenite, citrine, smoky quartz . . . name something, and I bet it's here. A regular-looking lady has come out from the back, where, surely, more mysteries must be hidden. She smiles and offers me help if I need it. Her hair is long and graying, and in that regard, she looks the part. I thank her, but I say that I am just looking right now. I want to take all this in. Frankly, I'm not sure what to even ask. About thirty questions boil up, really, but I feel like I might sound dumb or silly. Two of the questions are: Do you have a significant other who is cool with all this? And, are partners like that really out there? If they really exist, I want a concrete example.

I turn slowly to the white wire CD rack behind me, noticing the poster near the door of three pyramids looking beautiful and regal in the sunlight, all ancient and mysterious. I think maybe that's what inspired the store name. Annie is getting heavier by the second. I brought her little snack trap, a double-handled cup with a Tupperware lid that has slits for tiny fingers, just for this. Goldfish await to let Mama shop—to let Mama witch shop.

I notice that there is a small card table set off at the front window, to my right. It is covered by a tapestry and has folding chairs on either side. It looks like it is all ready for a crystal ball reading or some tarot cards to be whipped out. It's a perfect Annie spot: out of toddler reach for anything but maybe a few books and odds and ends, but she would have to work for those.

I put her down, and I feel thirty pounds lighter. I try to see what all witchy things consist of. Maybe this is what my home would look like were I to go whole hog witchified. There are wind chimes hanging through the center of the store, over the glass shelves—chimes of all shapes and sizes, and some that even look Native American. Behind the CD rack is another white wire rack for cards, and it is probably only about a quarter full. The cards are all illustrations of goddesses or women running through nature, things of that ilk. I go back to the first aisle and see that almost the entire left wall is covered with hooks, from each of which hang small plastic baggies with different herbs or ingredients. I wonder if they have Dragon's Blood? There are more things I have never heard of than of things I have. This is way out of my witch league.

Behind me are candles and oils. That's more like it. Each candle has a little sign set up next to its box, revealing the magic that the color and essence it contains is believed to purport. I choose a few votives. I know that at least I don't have to worry about hiding these. Through the years I have been the sole candle consumer and user in our house.

I set the votives on the counter and smile delicately at the woman working. I should just talk to her. Usually, I can strike up a convo with anyone. It's a rare day that I go into a public bathroom without chatting to another gal. Of course, that would be especially if I'm at a bar and there is alcohol involved. Maybe that's a big part of it.

Anyway, the woman gives her own version of the delicate smile, the store proprietor version, and I move on to my business and she to hers. With a quick glance in Annie's direction to make sure she is minding her own business as well, which she is, I set about checking out more of the store.

Underneath the oils and candles are a lot of bells of all different sizes, mostly brass. That seems to go with the wind chimes in some way. Maybe it's about meditative sound? Not sure. I'd like it if it were about ringing the bell for service from your man, but I suspect that isn't it at all. At the top of the shelf, nearer to the CD rack, is a cup of feathers—large, beautiful plumes in every bright color you can imagine. Annie would like these too much, I am afraid. She is already staring in the direction of the five or six peacock feathers in a container on the side windowsill. I know I don't have too much longer to linger without distraction.

I walk around the CDs and cards to the other side of the glass shelves. I am surprised to find a low rack of clothing back there. The owner really packs a lot of variety in a small space. Maybe it's because there aren't any big-box chain stores for mystical adventurers. The clothes are not my style, I surmise. I am not the least bit surprised. Maybe these are supposed to be ritual garments or something like that. There's material with circles dyed on them. There are folded tapestries nearby, too, and some kind of bandana-looking bits of fabric stacked on shelves near the clothing rack. More candles and oils fill the space as I walk toward the display cases near the cash register. I hear rustling, toddler talk, and the familiar call of "Mama" from behind me. Annie toddles up to join me and look in on the cases.

In the case by the right corner, in front of the door to the back room, there are crystals, crystal balls, fancy and elaborate and beautiful geodes, and stands for all the different ones. I like some of the larger crystals. They're lovely, and I find myself wanting to stare into them. Gaze, if you will. Funny! Maybe it is some natural inclination as humans that we have, to gawk and get mesmerized by shimmery crystals; maybe it is part of our animal natures, being attracted to shiny objects, like a cat or a raccoon.

I take a look at the prices. Holy shit, are crystals expensive! The one I like, a smaller one that sits on a stand, is a $160. The hanging ones are $25, $45. The baskets with the descriptions that I saw are way less, but they don't catch the light like these do.

I look up to the brass and golden goddess statues on shelves behind the counter. There they sit, beckoning my inner goddess nature to come out. I look down at the little person beside me, the little girl staring into the case, enchanted by the sparkling crystals before her. I can't help but think of her goddess nature. I question my own; I wonder if I have one. I wonder if it exists, or maybe it just disappeared after years of non-use. But if someone ever tried to tell me that this beautiful little creature, this endearing and precious life standing below me, didn't have a goddess nature, or that one day she would lose it, I would probably just laugh at the ridiculousness of that. No way. She has it, and she always will. If I can believe that about her, then why wouldn't it also be true for me, her mother? Rearranging thoughts and putting them in the context of Annie when I am down on myself always makes such a huge difference in the way I think.

So fine then, I am a goddess. And this woman nearby is, too. If I asked her, she would tell me, I imagine, that the goddess is within all of us—probably even men. They probably even have the masculine and the feminine within them. I laugh inside thinking of telling that to Pete. He wouldn't have any of that. He would think that was ridiculous. He would probably even think that having it within me was stupid, and that if I wanted to believe it, he would shake his head and laugh or scoff. Or both.

Maybe sometimes, I think to myself, I don't give him enough credit. Maybe I need to open up about all this stuff and tell him what I believe, to just go for it. There was the time in the car so long ago, when breezes and words all flowed so freely between us. He is different now, though. He sees life a certain way. He has a picture of the "should be" and I have a picture of the "could be." Once upon a time we had fun and talked. Those days seem so distant now. I wish I could talk to him. But then another part of me, a part that knows him and knows him very well, speaks up, telling me that I know what that would bring. He would think that was false; he would hate it; he would chastise me. I don't know if I have just developed this fear of him over time or if I really do know him and my not telling him and how I feel about life and the mysterious is founded in reality. Not that fear can't be founded in reality. I just wonder if, deep down, he would want me this unhappy—if he would want me to be this dissatisfied with our relationship and his treatment of me. I think maybe he is overpowered by the Christian indoctrination of being *the man*, who deserves a submissive and obedient woman—not a strong woman who stands up in her own goddess nature.

Strong women have always seemed to freak him out. He cannot stand Madonna. He is disgusted by Iman and thinks she is unattractive. He dislikes Bette Midler, Cher, Oprah, Tina Fey. I mean, Tina Fey? It's because she is a liberal, partly. All these women are nothing like his mother. And neither am I.

His mother is godly and obedient. Not that she isn't strong; on the contrary. But she didn't work outside her home (except at the church), and she raised four children. She keeps the home as it should be and she works hard for the Lord. She is the picture of what the quintessential 1950s American housewife role should be. Her family has a minivan and a Volvo. That's totally cool. It's just that I am not her. I am going nuts in this role.

All these thoughts prompted by those goddess statues. I want to tell the woman here what those just inspired in me, but something tells me she already knows.

I am too embarrassed at my own ignorance to ask what the silver goblets and chalices in the case below her are used for. Some kind of sacred something, some sort of ritual, I suppose. My parents used to have some. I wonder where those are? I have a moment where I imagine my parents engaged in some pagan ritual straight from *The Da Vinci Code*, and that makes me smile at its ridiculousness.

Amulets and jewelry round out the selection below the glass. Beautiful and intricately cast silver pieces sit untouched and lovely, waiting for their wearer to appear and take them home.

I finally see a crystal that I think might be right for me. I spotted a tiny basket that specified celestite, for new beginnings. Each is $3. It is soft and feels good in my hand. I take it, and I figure it will do if I believe. I want to believe.

I pay for my candles and crystal and thank the woman. Leaving, I take a last glance around at the mortar and pestle sets, the pentacles on the wall, the images of the moon, the wall of ingredients and herbs, and all the things that can be made into magic with the right touch.

I take Annie's hand and exit the store. I am happy with what I have discovered here—all those ancient symbols and ideas and items. Those things have been with humans for probably thousands of years—longer than Christianity has been with us. These magical items hold history within them and have long been a part of the history of humanity and will be for many years to come. There are most likely more people than we know keeping the traditions alive.

I leave feeling more emboldened and empowered. I anticipate a day when I can go to a place like this, come home, and tell whoever I am with. I am not imagining Pete in this scenario. I note that to myself but gloss over it. I tell that person all about it. I relax and am who I am. I wonder if I will ever be a woman who embraces pentacles, but I could be if I wanted, and that person next to me would understand and let me be. I anticipate a day when I have freedom, true freedom, which to me means responsibility but also the power to embrace who you are. I only will be able to allow myself to be that, but also others in my life will not be bothered by it.

It's funny how people can be as evangelical as they want and as right-wing Christian, and we are all expected to swallow it. We are expected to allow them to have their strong beliefs, and they have the freedom to pursue it. But bring out something like this, and it can draw fire. Fire and brimstone!

I want to love this goddess, this intuition, and cultivate her and be who or what I already am. I want it for me, and I want it for this small little baby goddess I have the amazing blessing of cultivating. I take a deep breath and give Annie an extra squeeze as I slip her into her car seat, knowing that all these things are possible. If I envision it, it can become real. I take another deep breath that fades into a wistful sigh, and I hope that this is all true. *Please let it be true.*

 *Eight*

HOPE SPRINGS ETERNAL.

Xander and I sit facing each other, each with a glass of wine to our right and the crystal between us, not quite sure what to do next. I have enlisted him to help me with all of this, probably because he is the most pagan person I know despite his Catholic upbringing.

Even though I have been studying up on the internet, I have some doubt and a sense of trepidation. It's the same nagging fear and worry as always—that I not only will be perceived as some kind of morally horrific, spiritually bereft mother, but that maybe, maybe, *I actually am.*

I managed to buy a book called *The Good Spell Book* because I figured that had a nice energy about it. When I was buying it, I had some fearful moments when I thought someone I knew might see me browsing through the occult section in BookPeople and bust me by telling Pete or something. My fear raises its head once again.

"Should I wiggle my nose?" Xander lifts his finger to his nose at the same time he raises his wine to his full lips, now with a smile spreading across them.

"Maybe." I try to do it. "Maybe it'll inspire us."

We are here for him. His business is having some trouble and Pete is out tonight for a friend's bachelor party. I am thrilled and ready. Annie's in bed, and we are secretly meeting, covertly, to do a little money spell and see what happens.

It is a waxing moon tonight (I checked), which portends growth in finances if the spell is cast then. The book insists that this urgent money spell, as it is called, must be performed at midnight—"the witching hour," as the book calls it. I think that we have gotten lucky in finding a night that Pete is gone when we can actually do this.

First, we are supposed to light one white votive candle representing each hundred or thousand dollars you need. Xander's business needs a lot, so we got ten candles, each representing $10,000.

We sit down at 11:45 as instructed by the book. I light a separate gold candle, one that I bought at the witch store that I am excited to finally use. It says it will give power to the money candles and enable us to see what we are doing, since we have turned all the lights off in the house. I think that is very possibly the more important use of it at this moment.

The light from the candle reflects off the glass table. I see Xander's face before me, the flicker adding a spooky look to him and a glint to his eyes.

As instructed in the book, we say a little prayer for a circle of gold light to be placed around us for protection and a circle of blue light for healing. This amounts to us laughing and basically saying words because we never quite know what we are doing. I am imagining his business in these circles as well.

It then instructs us to pick up a votive and light it from the main candle. I have put them all on a large dish in a circle, with the main candle in the center. I make Xander do this part. We already went over what we were going to do, and he remembers it well. He picks up his first candle and holds it over the lit gold candle in the center.

"This candle represents $10,000," he says.

We sound so greedy. But really, we aren't. His business is struggling, and he needs a major infusion of cash. He has a meeting with the bank on Monday morning and I figure this will hold over through Sunday to help him.

He sets down the first white votive and repeats the same thing with each one. "This candle represents $10,000. . . . This candle represents $10,000. . . . This candle represents $10,000."

He does this over and over until there is heat and a bright glow between us. I am looking at him over the glow and smiling. I like having a partner in crime or, I should say, a willing participant.

Our last step is to say a prayer explaining that the money is necessary, that we are not being greedy. I prod Xander to go ahead and say this prayer.

He begins. "Oh light and love," he says hurriedly, with a nonchalant tone to his voice, "Um . . . I ask that this money be brought to my business not out of greed but instead out of a true and very real need." He chuckles and continues. "A very real need."

Briefly his left hand goes to his mouth in a pensive gesture, and I can hear him breathing. He removes his hand from in front of his face and interlaces his fingers in a true asking and prayer pose. He continues, "We genuinely ask for help with this money from our hearts. This money would lift a burden off of me—not entirely, but so much so that I could work and focus with a more comforted mind. I pray and ask for the blessing to come down upon us and heal this monetary wound."

I give him a look of approval and surprise at that last turn of phrase. He looks serious.

"Should I say Amen?" he quietly inquires.

"How about we both say 'Blessed Be'?"

"OK. Blessed Be."

I repeat after him. "Blessed Be."

"OK."

I nod my head and smile. We both are kind of surprised at how easy that was. It has been kind of fun to follow and perform a little ritual. "OK," I echo.

I turn on the living room lamp again and look at the time. It is just now midnight. We are supposed to leave the candles lit until they burn themselves out. I am not sure how I am going to pull that off with Pete getting home within a couple of hours, but I am going to try.

"What if Pete comes home and blows out the candles?" I ask.

"Maybe I could take them home with me."

"I don't know. Driving with those sounds like a bad idea. I'm not sure why but it sounds dangerous, cruising up the highway with open flames on the floorboard beside you."

"Yeah, I'm sure, it's all smoky and bright inside there, then you get pulled over and arrested for driving with an open flame."

"And what if you had to stop for gas?" I laugh and sip the cabernet, which brings warmth to the inside of my chest and belly. It feels good and numbing and comforting.

"Yeah, that'd be great." He mimics talking to a gas station attendant. "I'd like $10 on pump number five. Oh, wait, that one's on fire now from my candles. Can I do pump two?"

"It'd be like that scene in *Zoolander*."

"When they have the gas fight!"

I start to sing. "'Wake me up, before you go-go . . .'"

We both laugh at the memory of *Zoolander* and then park it on the couch, candles burning on the table behind us, hopefully sending smoke signals to the powers that be for him and some money. I am really just curious about the spell and what can be, *if* it can be. I want to see what happens. The title of the spell, "Urgent Money Spell," intrigued me. I thought maybe then I could actually see some results, since I hadn't seen any from my own spell yet. There had been no giant shift in my life. There was a nag in me, though, on how we were going to keep these candles lit through the night. I hoped that since they were small votives that they would burn out fairly quickly, but they weren't making any big steps toward that at the moment.

We hung out and had another glass of wine, then Xander declared his exhaustion and decided to head home, after we had talked about his business, people we knew, and all sorts of topics, with the exception of my stupid life, which I would change the subject on because I didn't even feel like it was worth talking about.

"You sure you don't want to drive with these candles?"

"I probably wouldn't even have to use my headlights."

"Or maybe just one of them."

"Yeah! And that way, if I got pulled over, I could just say that I was trying to save energy!"

"Trying to go green?"

We laugh and kiss on the lips, a highlight to our relationship for me. I see him off and come back in, bothered still by those candles that are creeping down at a pace slower than a snail's. I could hide them upstairs. But what if they lit the house on fire? Then the fire would start upstairs with Annie. That's out. I could sleep next to them, but what about when Pete gets home. What then? Anyway, these things provide way too much light and would most likely be disturbing. I ponder. I finally decide to put the dish with the lit candles in the fireplace, right underneath the grate. I text Pete saying that Annie is good, I went to bed, and please don't blow out the candles, I would like for them to go out on their own. I hope that does it. I am sure that I will get questions, but I will deal with those in the morning.

I hit the bed, wondering about how I will explain the candles. They are a dead giveaway that we have been up to something. I hid the book before I laid down. Even after all my big talk, the best I could come up with was a shoebox again. That was partly why I felt safe buying that book—because it is so petite and hidable.

I fall asleep hoping that the answer will befall me in dreams. I fantasize through the night that I tell Pete that we were casting a spell to help Xander's business, and in my fantasy, he understands and doesn't care. Everybody is all pleasant with one another, and we are happy, children are fed, bills are paid, and things are easy.

I must have been sleeping very hard because I never hear Pete come home. Usually the large moan of the garage door wakes me, but tonight, I lay restful and tired. Dreams of a peaceful house and a wonderful life comfort me in my rest. I think of happy times and of someone like Xander, someone who loves me and lets my candles burn as long as they need to.

I wake up to the a stirring on the baby monitor the next morning, the sweet coos of a stinky but cute child standing up in her crib, waiting for Mama to come in—that one person in her life who means the most. Then, I look at the clock. It's only 4:22. Way too early this morning. Annie can go right back to sleep. The bed is empty next to me, and I wonder if Pete even came home. Surely he would have called if he had gotten drunk and decided to crash somewhere?

My mind is full of questions. I spring up, throw on my sweats (my house uniform), and get moving, first into the living room hoping to find him on the sofa. The candles are a mess of dried wax, all burned out of their own accord. Haha! I have a little rejoice-party in my head. Small victories. This one is very small. Of all nights for him not to come home, I couldn't have wished for a better one. My candles, or rather, Xander's candles, burned out on their own, and I am thrilled. Of course, I wonder if that even makes a difference, but I am sure if not the *negative*, then the *non-interested* breath of Pete blowing them out would not have helped the energy we were promoting.

I have a missed call on my phone from a number I don't recognize. I am really wondering about Pete right now. I wonder if he was in an accident; I wonder if he is dead. Not that I want him dead, but I feel a little indifferent to that prospect. This is not the driving fear that one should probably feel when thinking of the death of their life partner. That person should complete you, shouldn't they, like the movie with Tom Cruise? Shouldn't the thought of their death bring a feeling of losing part of yourself, the best part of yourself? But I am cool. I think that I would feel relieved. That should indicate to me that something is terribly amiss and a-miss-ing in this picture. It's not what you should feel. Not in the least.

So I see that the call came in around 3:23 a.m. I think, *Fuck it, I will call it and see. It might be Pete. Wait. There's a voicemail.* I listen. The soothing woman announcer recites the same unfamiliar number, and then the message starts.

"Hey, Veronica, it's John Pearson," the deep, smoky voice begins, its slight slur betraying the alertness accompanying his tone.

I know John. He is the reason Pete was out last night with those guys for that bachelor party. Pete was really there to try to get some contacts for his mortgage business—to get some income flowing in this thing he calls a business, anyway. I am starting to really feel alert now. My ears are pricked up and listening intently.

"Um, I am calling because Pete asked me to. We got pulled over and he was brought in for DWI."

Arrested! A nice way of saying arrested! Holy fucking shit. Goddamnit. Fuck. Obscenities are rushing through my head. So much for making money on this excursion. I keep listening over the trill of curse words running around in my mind. I am fucking pissed.

"We have it handled right now, but call me on this number as soon as you can. We will bail him out tonight. He didn't want you to panic with the baby and all, so call me, and I will let you know what's going on. But don't worry. Right now, we are here at the station where he is and trying to work to get him out. Paul Sheffield was with us and he's an attorney and has a friend who handles DWI cases so he called that guy for Pete and he is working on it already, so we didn't want you to worry. OK. Sooooo . . ." His voice trails off. I hear phone movement and can't understand what he's saying. Then he comes back coherently. "Call this number. Thanks, I will talk to you later."

I delete the message. I just stand there, staring at myself in the mirror in the hallway, but really just staring right through it. Thoughts are no longer racing through my mind. I feel a little blank. I feel a little dead inside.

I walk back to the bedroom and check the monitor. It seems like sometimes Annie can sense when someone is awake, so I am mentally crossing my fingers that she is back to sleep. I hear nothing from her room upstairs. I still hold my phone in my hand as I sit on the bed, gearing up to call John back. I bet the car is impounded. At least these guys were with him. They have families, too, and maybe they will have that old "coulda been me" feeling and will help him—or will help us—through the morning. I shake my head. I sense that I keep unconsciously doing that. I feel it shaking again, in full disapproving mode.

Good god, of course that could have been me, a hundred times over. I actually got pulled over and drunk-tested when

Annie was about four months old. I had been out and my tolerance was not what it used to be. I should have gone to jail. I played the breastfeeding card, and played it hard. I lied to the female officer and told her that I had a baby at home—see the empty car seat in the back?—and I couldn't drink much at all, in fact I had only had two drinks (lie!) all night, because I was breastfeeding. I had really had about seven drinks. So irresponsible. But the suburbs are sometimes too far to take an Uber or taxi, you rationalize, especially when you feel broke and know it would cost nearly $40. The reasoning that it is so much fucking cheaper than a DWI doesn't really factor in at that particular point.

Anyway, somehow, someway, I passed that test, the watching of the light, the walking of a straight line, and she scolded me and let me go. What a sobering moment that was, in more ways than the obvious. I don't want to be a hypocrite, because Lord knows I have zero room to be one after all the times I have driven past the limit and tempted fate—way too many times, way, way too many. But yet I feel like judging. I feel like being pissed.

Probably the one thing that Pete needs right now is compassion. I might have it if his drunk driving wasn't completely worse than mine. He will regularly have a couple of beers and drive with Annie in the car. He will drink and drive without a thought, every week, several times a week. I hate it, I beg him not to, and I tell him he is stupid. I catch my own "I told you so" rhetoric I am spewing, but I am letting it flow, letting it flood my thoughts. The current gets stronger the more I allow it to roll and tide. Waves of strong emotion and anger fill my head. I am sick of him and his immaturity and fucking sick of all of this shit with him. I feel steely; I feel cold and bitter and just plain mad.

The phone still sits in my hand, my finger on the button, ready to call John back. I know I need to calm down. It isn't like I am red-faced and poised to yell or anything of the sort. That has never been my operational mode. I know what I need to give Pete. But sometimes it is so incredibly hard to really step outside of things and give that other person what he or she needs. Especially when you are so close in it, so affected by it, and you know that whatever the problem is will affect you and your life personally. But this affects his life much more than mine, I suppose. I will be financially affected, and it will hurt, but that will most likely be the worst of it for me. Pete will have to deal with the lawyers, the courts, the embarrassment. Of course, I suppose that nowadays it is pretty run of the mill, that everyone understands. I mean, celebrities get arrested for driving on something all the time.

I make the call. John finally answers after the fourth ring. A little part of me was rooting for voicemail, probably as a kind of avoidance mechanism. I take a deep breath as I hear the hello on the other end of the line.

"Hi, John," I say softly, with gratitude in my voice, hopefully covering up some of my other feelings. "It's Veronica Cantrell, Pete's wife?" I am not sure what else to say at this point, so I just stop.

"Oh, hey, Veronica," John sounds tired, yet much more lucid than the last call. "I'm glad you got my message. Apparently it costs a bunch to do the call from jail these days or something and it's really complicated, so we thought it was better to try and reach you this way."

"Are you still there at the station? What do I need to do?"

"Well, unfortunately, there isn't very much you can do right now, 'cause he has to go in front of the judge and that won't happen until six. But Paul called his attorney friend, and he has already worked on setting up bail and everything. I managed to get Pete's wallet so I used one of his credit cards. I hope that is OK and all."

"Yeah, of course." I have a debt-flash whip through my mind. *Oh fucking well.*

John goes on. "He's fine though. He'll just have to stay in there a little while longer."

"Are you still there?"

"No, we just called a cab and are headed home. Paul was with me and Pete when it happened."

"What *did* happen? So you were with Pete when he got stopped?" Dumb question, I guess. But it's four thirty in the morning. I ask stupid questions at that time of day.

"Yeah. God, it was just one of those little things, you know, a dumb little mistake, we had left the bar we were at—"

The question, "Titty bar?" comes up in my mind, and I smile a little half-smile, because I hope that Pete at least got to see some hot girls and tits and ass before going into the pokey, but I refrain from asking and figure the answer would have been yes.

"So Pete was going to take us to our cars which were still down on Fourth Street. He was at Lamar and Fifth and just barely cut this guy off the get-into-the-left-turn lane to turn onto Fifth Street and of course, wouldn't you know it, it was a cop. We were so fucking pissed."

"Did he blow?"

"Oh, god no. He even did well on all the tests, I mean, he passed 'em," John says, with his indignant West Texas twang kicking in. "I think they were just determined to take him in."

Yeah, right. I am sure that Pete was totally sober—not. I am sitting straight up on my bed. My feet are freezing, and my nose is like an ice cube. I wish I was warm and not having to deal with this, but I know that's not the case. I suck it up and tuck my toes under the warmth of the duvet and blanket, rubbing the tip of my nose with my free hand and feeling the lids of my eyes droop at the tiring prospect of dealing with this situation. I sigh.

John goes on. "We were told to take a cab home, but we just made an executive decision to head over there and help him out, especially since he had set his wallet down in the car when he got his license out. I just held onto that for him, and I still have it. They had a tow truck come, and his truck was impounded."

"Geez. How do we get that, I wonder?"

"I think the attorney can help you. His name is Alan Bettis, and he's supposed to be this really good DWI guy in town. He apparently knows a lot. He does this all the time, and he can tell you everything. I have his card here just so you can get the number."

"Thanks."

He gives me the number, and I feel a chill as I scramble up, grabbing a pen out of the top drawer of my antique vanity table where there are some Post-it notes, too. I jot down Alan's name and number and dread that call now ahead of me, looming in the early morning.

We wrap up our call. I thank John profusely for all he has done. He concludes by confirming exactly what I had suspected.

"You know, it coulda been any one of us, god, you know? It coulda been me, so it was the least we can do. It really sucks that the night had to end this way, but, y'know." He trails off with that last bit, leaving whatever it is that I know to my imagination. But I understand. I do know.

So I make the follow-up calls. I call the attorney and get a little more information. I find out fun stuff like how to get the impounded truck and how I need cash for that and how Pete will go in front of the judge and how this is all routine. I think, *Routine for who? This is certainly not part of my regular routine.* I find myself getting up, pacing around the house, and watching the morning tick by and the sun rise little by little, with its early light casting a gray haze over the house and reminding me that there will once again be light in life, no matter how dark things can seem. I know I am being a little dramatic with that. I know that there are a lot of things that could be worse. He could have hurt someone, which would be nightmarishly worse. He could have been hurt himself, or dead—would that be worse? *Yes*, I tell myself, *yes, it would have been much worse*, and I am surprised at my own conviction and sentiment in the face of what I had thought days ago.

I pace and ponder those thoughts about what Pete will need today. I am prepared to step outside this situation, to give him the compassion that I know he will need. I imagine that he will feel embarrassed and sheepish and puny and tired and all those awful, shameful emotions that could possibly come up after an event of this magnitude. I really want to give what he needs. I want to be that kind of friend, to treat him as I would a best pal, to give him the break I would cut for Gin or Xander or even his friend John, had it been him.

That is tough to do for the father of your child, that person you tend to expect more from. It's that one person in life that you hope will rise up and be the inspiration and example that you dream of. But we all make mistakes, have missteps and problems, and do stupid shit on occasion. Maybe the example we set can be more in how we handle ourselves through those times.

Or maybe this is my chance to set an example in how I behave, how I treat someone else. That thought softens up my bristly back almost immediately. This might be my chance to show him, and to show myself, that we can treat people the right way even when they make decisions that could bug us but really, in the end, don't affect us. Like the way I am with this whole witch thing. Maybe it will even out our playing field, so to speak. Maybe I can start to talk to him about what I want to pursue and study at the moment, to tell him that I am interested in nature and all those earthy ways of connecting to the world and to others. Maybe by showing him that what he went through affects him more and that I understand that, I can help him become more compassionate toward me.

I feel hopeful. I feel like I did when Obama was up for election the first time, like there may be a light at the end of this tunnel, however faint. There may be a shot at what I am in need of, too. Maybe we can reconnect, Pete and me, maybe it will be like a rom-com, where opposites live side by side and make it work with an understanding of each other.

I stare out at the dawn and hope that the sunrise is a metaphor for where my life is going, beyond Pete, after Pete. A little voice in the back of my head tells me that nature is symbolizing the dawn of a new life for me, a new day on my own life. *Nothing against Pete, but it's about you.* I convert and contort that voice's words to match the ones that go with what I was already thinking about me and Pete. I grasp at that hope, and I think that maybe he is someone that I can talk to after all.

 # Nine

THOSE THREE LITTLE WORDS.

I have been up for four hours already, and it's barely eight o'clock. Annie is loaded up in the car, and it is a blustery Sunday morning. A cold wind blew in last night, finally. My allergies are running rampant; the nose blowing and sneezing make me sound especially charming today. I have a moment and wonder what I would feel like if I were still pregnant, if I'd feel tired, worn out, sick. Or, maybe I'd feel happy, glowing—or maybe trapped.

Annie is perky and adorable and snuggly, dressed in her light pink fleece sweat suit. I am in my black Old Navy workout uniform, a burgundy scarf twisted around my neck as chicly as I could get it to look. I figured we should make an effort for Pete, for his sake, just to make him feel like someone gives a shit. I run get some cash and am all poised and ready to go get him and the car. I have it fairly well sorted out and have already learned more than I bargained for since I woke up at the crack of nothing but darkness this morning.

I still feel the hope from earlier that this event might set a new tone for me and Pete. I think part of that might be because I suspect sometimes he thinks I am a little stupid and ditzy and flighty and generally not that smart; he tends to think that of anyone who has politically liberal views. That's fucking annoying. But now he is the stupid one, not that I am labeling or pointing fingers, but still he did the fucking up and maybe he will feel more like I am an equal, even if he does think I am not all that smart. That might be the crux of this whole problem. Or at least, it's at the base of it all. My eyes dart around a little. I am disturbed by my own thoughts, and I suspect that if I said them out loud to anyone (except Pete) that they would think I was nuts for staying in a relationship that was hardly a relationship at all. It's unbalanced, unfair— the Fox News of relationships.

I never, ever dreamed that this would be my life. Sure, I dreamed of marrying a handsome guy and having a home, I guess. Actually, I am not sure that I ever even envisioned any of that. I know that I never thought that I would be married before thirty, certainly not at twenty-four. I never thought I would live in suburbia and have moments of madness when I considered the benefits of owning a minivan.

I really thought that I would die before I was thirty. I simply couldn't see past that number. There has always been an event or age in my life that I couldn't see past, so I just figured that I was going to die before it occurred. Probably a symptom of not wanting to live life on my own terms or of being scared of taking care of my own shit.

Then that event or age would occur, and I would move on. I'd have to readjust to not seeing past the next mark. I never could imagine myself actually even graduating from high school, so I became convinced that I was going to drop dead before that last day of senior year. Then I lived to party right through it. So I thought, *Oops! It must be college that I won't make it though. Wrong graduation.* Then I managed to stay breathing through that milestone. And on and on it went. It might even go so far back as to when I was ten or so; I do distinctly remember a point in fifth grade when I wasn't turning in my spelling homework at all and was getting zeroes. I thought I would never have to deal with any of the repercussions. I thought I might have something whisk me away from it all, and then it wouldn't matter that I hadn't done any spelling work. Maybe this is some form of denial. I should probably look into that in a psychological sense. I don't do it anymore. Now I just expect others to die, apparently. I cringe.

The attorney had said he was going to help Pete get all squared away. He told me to just drive up and pick him up in front of the police station at Eighth and I-35, in the front, where he would be waiting. I stop for Starbucks to brighten his world just a little bit. The attorney was quite right; there was Pete, loitering with him outside the jail and police station, waiting for me, Pete looking cold and tired and older, hands in the pockets of his only pair of Diesel jeans and shirt and dark navy velvet blazer looking a little suspect but not too out of place. That's probably the good thing about being a guy going to jail rather than a girl. You get to still walk out in fairly comfortable and appropriate attire. If I had gone to jail after a bachelorette party, I would probably be looking like a sex worker at this point: eye makeup smeared, no lipstick, fuck-me heels and a short skirt or too tight top or some other wildly inappropriate item of clothing that screamed, "Yes, yes, I have been up all night, and now I look rode hard and put up wet. Feast your eyes."

But there he stands, wearing only slightly identifiable evening party wear, looking pitiful nonetheless, and I don't blame him.

Poor guy. I do feel bad for him. I don't care that I will bear the brunt of work with Annie today. He has had a rough night, and I want to be that compassionate soul who is there to help, not to hinder, not to hound or nag or beat him up.

He opens the car door, and Alan and I get a quick formal introduction. Everyone is all nice and briefly chatty; I find myself trying to be giggly to lift the mood a little. It's awkward. I stop. Annie is talking about Daddy in the backseat and Pete hops into the passenger's seat, happy to be there and in some vehicle to take him away from all of this, all of which must be fading into what seems like a bad dream already.

"Hi babe," I say softly. I lean over to give him a kiss.

"Hi." He kisses me back. Just a little peck, and my ubernose quickly senses that there was no teeth brushing at the jail last night. I keep that one to myself. Talk about rubbing salt in the wound. *Wow, how was jail? You breath is horrible, by the way! And is that BO and old booze I smell on you?*

"How ya doing, babe?" I ask.

"How do you think?!" he replies, hostility seeping out from the words.

I instantly feel a pang of sadness. I reach over and pet the back of his neck, those soft little baby animal hairs cut short and downy.

He pulls his head forward a little bit, away from my hand. "I'm sorry. I didn't mean to snap at you. I just mean that this fucking sucks. How do you think I'm doing?"

I bite my tongue on asking him not to drop the word fuck in earshot of little ears back in the backseat. Whatever, for now. I want him soothed, if not for his sake, then for my own selfish reasons, to make my and Annie's lives that much more peaceful and calm. I put my hand down and rest it on his leg. I stay quiet. I am not sure what I can say to him right now without upsetting things, so I just let it be.

"We can talk whenever you want." I take a breath and say the right thing. "I love you, and I am glad that you're OK."

He makes a pitiful face, tucking his lips into one another and nodding a small nod. "Thanks." He pauses. "Thanks for coming to get me, too."

I can't resist a little laugh. "Babe! Of course! Silly." I let the moment rest. Then I add, to rub in what a good wife I am, "I brought you a Starbucks." I tap the lid of his in the other cup holder bedside me.

"I smell it. You're the best wife in the world."

He gives me a sad but sweet smile, and I smile back. This makes me feel good. I think that there really might be hope after all. I think we will be able to talk today. I think he is loving me for who I am and realizing that he isn't perfect either, but it doesn't matter at all. That perfect façade that he wants to project is not important in life. This DWI may be insanely expensive, but something good will come out of it. And really, what good would it do for me to beat him up about it?

He turns back to Annie. "Hi, Sweetheart! Daddy is so glad to see you!"

Annie speaks some baby talk back that sounds like "Hi, Daddy!" if that's what you want it to be, and seems overall thrilled to see her daddy.

We drive, quietly, through quiet and empty streets of Austin. I have already nailed down where his car is. Although it is far, we don't live too many miles away from it. He asks if I know, I tell him I do, and we are headed down there, far, far south in Austin, almost out of the city limits. As we are getting closer, he starts to talk and tell me about the arrest and jail and all the fun he had.

"I still can't believe that cop brought me in. I wasn't even drunk!"

Uh-huh. Sure you weren't. Just like everybody else who gets a DWI. Stone cold sober. I am really honing my tongue-biting skills lately.

He continues, "I was taking Paul and John to their cars." He stares out the window as he talks, watching the sun reflect off the windows of the buildings as we pass them. "They were parked downtown."

"Where were you coming from?"

A pause. "Yellow Rose."

"That's what I figured," I reply, stifling a smile. Sober coming from a strip joint, I am so sure. The times I have been, I have had to get drunk. Everyone with me did too.

"But really, I shouldn't have been arrested."

He isn't acting belligerent, but I can tell that he feels strongly about this. I feel like blurting out, "Who are you kidding, and how many times have you gotten away with it when you deserved to be thrown in jail for three days?" But I don't. I listen. I nod. I tug on my scarf around my neck and internally, I roll my eyes.

"That cop was just ready to bring someone in. To like, meet a quota or something." He takes a long draw on his coffee, and I do the same. "I passed every test he gave me, totally. The attorney said that they probably have it all on video and that could work in my favor, so, you know, that's good."

His bristles are softening, I think, since he realizes that I am not going to argue with him.

"Man. I did so good, too! I really thought he was gonna let me go."

He sighs, and the odor of stale booze drifts through the car. I hold my breath for a second to let it pass, resisting the urge to crack the window for a second. He shakes his head, very slightly, glances at his disposable coffee cup, and resumes staring out the window, his right hand coming up to his face and massaging his forehead. I pat his leg and stare straight ahead.

We remain silent for the rest of the trip. I decide that I will hear the story over time, although I somewhat feel like I already know it. I mostly feel like I don't care. I don't need to hear any more of it. I am slightly curious about what jail was like, but I have heard stories from other friends and I am sure that his experience will come out over time. I am surprised, however—surprised at myself for how little I care to hear about what he went through. I feel mildly contemptuous toward him, but I hide it. Or, maybe I not so much hide it but am ashamed of it, because it's low to feel that toward your husband when he needs you. It's low, I know, but sometimes I just want honesty out of him, for him to go, "Yeah, I'm an idiot, and boy did I fuck up. I had no business behind the wheel. Why didn't we take a cab?" and hear him be just fucking real and honest. Because truly, I have sat with people who are drinking when I'm not, and they stink. There is no doubt in my mind that the inside of that truck when the window was rolled down for the cop stunk like an old hobo.

Pete has jumped into reading the directions and taken to telling me where to go. I try to tell him that I mapped it already and know where I am headed, but he directs me anyway and argues with a turn I make that I think is faster. It still gets us to the same place. He is too tired to argue very hard and the coffee hasn't fully kicked in yet, so that saves me some grief. I tried to be understanding, compassionate, and all that shit this morning, but now I am tired, too. I am losing patience with him for not being as humble or repentant as I think he should be.

We are finally here. I stop in front of the small structure where I assume from the bars on the outside that this is where they take the cash for the impounded cars. I give Pete the cash I have and get out with him, clutching the insurance paperwork and any car info we had, any- and everything, just so we could actually get the truck out. They search by VIN number and thankfully, everything goes smoothly. Pete gets the car, we share a cold, dry peck on the lips that neither of us really wants, and he is on his way and I am on mine.

"See you at home."

"K."

I get back into my car, where it's warm and the little face in the backseat is staring at me expectantly. I greet her and let her know we will see daddy at home. Unfortunately. So much for my commitment to not being bitchy. I feel it rising up within me. I know how I want to treat him, and I know how I would want to be treated, but it seems nearly impossible to muster. I think it might be wise to let all my bitchy feelings rise up right here in the car, where he isn't, and then leave them here. Maybe I can get them all out and then they will be gone. Or, maybe I will be feeding them and they will grow bigger.

Whatever the case, they're there, and they must get out. In my head, I suppress them no longer. The same thoughts and angry feelings that first emerged with the revelation of this situation arise. Maybe I am no better than Pete about putting on airs and acting fake, after the way I just acted toward him, which wasn't real. No, it was real, but he didn't act right back. I expected groveling, I expected humility, I expected penance or at least an attempt at it. I wanted him to acknowledge an error, a fuckup, to be real with me, of all people, and then with himself, but I didn't get any of that. I got denial. I got snapping. I got un-real, un-truth. Is this the kind of person I want?

Maybe it was just typical of someone dealing with the realities of going to jail. I've watched *Cops*. Aren't they all in some sort of denial? I like to think that if I were in that boat, I might go, at least after the fact, "Yeah, OK, I really shouldn't have been doing what I was doing. I really was fucked up, and there is no way on God's green earth that I would have passed a breathalyzer or a blood test. I deserved what I got. Chalk

one up for the 5-0. They caught me after all these years."
I like to think that I would be honest, shake my head, and
know I probably got what I deserved, what was in actuality
a long time coming. I like to think that's how it would have
gone, but maybe I would be sitting there in denial, too, bitter
that it was me driving and not my friend, which it could have
been if not for one teeny decision made earlier in the night.

I am not sure that Pete is even conscious of his own
denial. I wonder, when in that situation, if it isn't apparent that you are denying your own culpability. Or, is this a
developed personality trait? Is it a white, Gen-X symptom of
entitlement? He has to, deep down, be conscious of his own
responsibility, doesn't he? I think it would be impossible to
not know the truth in this, even if you deny it to yourself.
Maybe he should consider therapy. Isn't it psychosis to shield
your heart from the truth and continue that behavior for
extended periods of time? Isn't it just flat-out crazy?

My brain goes and goes, and I keep letting it run, halfway hearing the kids' music playing as background noise,
entertaining Annie in the back as Mama sits and stews and
stirs the pot of her own mind against the man she is supposed
to love.

I wonder if I am no better. I am the drunk, I am in denial
about who I am and how I am treated, and yet I expect to be
treated better.

We are sitting at a stoplight, and I decide to cast a spell.
A tiny voice inside me pipes up and begins a protest: *Who do
you think you are, to cast a spell? You aren't qualified! You
are a novice. Stop kidding yourself. Give this up. You won't
accomplish anything, even if you do try.* I find another voice.

Go fuck yourself, little voice, it says. *Everybody's gotta start someplace, and I trust my other voices more than you.*

Everything falls quiet. I imagine a blue light surrounding me and Annie, separately and together, smaller circles of light within one larger one. I close my eyes and imagine it hard, that this blue halo of light protects us from everything, guards us, and holds us close, each of us and us together. The car behind me taps their horn twice. I open my eyes quickly to the green light staring back at me, prompting me to get moving. I take a deep breath and go, calmly pressing the gas and holding onto this light, this protection.

Home isn't far now. We arrive behind Pete. I am not sure how he beats us home every single time, but it must be the fact that he drives entirely too fast. He zooms around in that big truck, throwing his weight around, usually because he's late but sometimes I think it also might be because he just likes driving fast.

He is already in the house when we open the garage. He is looking in the fridge and probably ready to shove the first thing he sees into his mouth. I have a little food leftover from our pre-money-spell dinner last night, and I offer it to him. My heart softens. There is still hope. There can still be happiness here, right? I watch him talk to Annie as they both look in the fridge, hanging out together. Pete is being incredibly sweet to her as she stands clutching her zebra in her little hand. I can never say he isn't good with her. He may not be that good with me, but he's great with her. My hope is reviving. I wouldn't say that it's off life support, but it's maybe starting to breathe on its own again.

I get out some toys for Annie and set them on the living

room floor. I grab a lighter to start the gas logs in the fireplace since it's still pretty cold out and to make it as sweet as possible in here for Pete, my jailbird, as welcoming and as homey as possible. I forgot that I have to do something with those candles that are still sitting, burned out, a beautiful mess of melted wax, in the fireplace. I pick up the dish and silently move it to the breakfast room, hoping not to raise any inquiries out of Pete but fully prepared with my bag of hope hanging on my hip, fully prepared to ease him into whatever we were up to, hopeful still that I can be just the teeniest bit truthful if he asks or seems interested.

I light the fire and sit on the floor with some toys, close enough to feel the warmth, dogs sniffing and interested in whether I have any food or not. Annie comes over and Pete stays in the kitchen, heating up last night's beautifully cooked leftover risotto I made that is some of the best comfort food ever.

The microwave finishes, and Pete walks into the living room through the breakfast room. I give a sidelong glance to see if he is looking at my candle mess. I think he saw it.

"What's that?" He asks, grabbing the remote and flipping on the TV, flopping down on the sofa, feet up on the ottoman.

"What?" I play dumb. Or better yet, I play nonchalant.

"Those candles all burned down?"

"Oh, I had those burning in the fireplace last night." I give a little laugh, as if to say, "Oh, aren't I silly!" and continue, "Xander was over here and his business is having some money problems, so we lit candles in sort of a, you know, please-rain-money-for-him kind of thing." I say all this pleasantly and softly and easily, like I have nothing to hide.

Pete frowns. "Like a witch thing? Like you're now trying to be a witch and cast a spell or something?"

"Don't Catholics light candles for stuff? Can't it be like a prayer?"

"Sounds different than that to me. Catholics do that in church." He takes an enormous bite and continues. "This sounds like you think you're in a movie or something. V, you're not starring in a remake of *The Craft*, OK?"

I give him a face. He knows I have always been drawn to the supernatural. It didn't used to bother him. Or did it, and I just wasn't paying attention? I give a look with my eyes under my brow and a little quick puff of a sigh. "I never said I was. I just was trying to help Xander in any way that I could think of, so we came up with this idea and just did something. What does it even matter?"

"It matters because—" He catches his rising tone and lowers it solely for Annie's sake, not for mine, I am sure. He goes on, softening his voice and dumbing it down for me, talking in the sweetest mean tone I can think of. "It matters because I don't want that in my house or around my daughter."

I roll my eyes, and I let him see it. "It's my house, too, and I wasn't doing anything wrong. Just helping my friend."

"And you know, that's another thing I've been think-ing about." I guess jail gave him time to think. "I let you be friends with him thinking that it was good for you, that it kept you having fun with fashion stuff, but he's not going to be welcome here if this what you guys are going to do."

My eyes grow huge, and I am shocked at his boldness. "You *let* me be friends with him?!"

"Yeah, well," he says, nodding and still sure of himself, never admitting a mistake or doubting himself a fraction, "maybe that came out a little strong, and I didn't mean for it to. I just meant that I was OK with you having that friendship with him but not when you are doing some candle-lighting ceremony for money that seems like some sort of spell in my house."

I clam up. I fall totally silent and angry and hurt. I focus on Annie, her little zebra stuffed animal, and the fishbowl toy that she can put balls in and out of. I smile a little at her and just play for a moment.

Several minutes pass.

"So what, now you're just not going to say anything?" He flips the channel to a fishing show.

I shrug and take my time with an answer. I don't really have anything to say. I tried to say what I was doing in a very light manner; not that what we were doing was all that heavy in the first place. But it failed miserably. So much for that life support. I feel this thing flatlining. I have no interest in speaking to him. All I get is shit. "Nothing to say." I can hear my voice, dripping with attitude.

Maybe I am being immature. But he isn't my dad, able to tell me who I can and cannot play with. Not that my dad ever had any luck with that one though, either. Besides, he has always acted like he loved Xander, palling around with him and even agreeing to make him Annie's godfather, content to hang out with him and having a good time and knowing Xander's family and everything. This is ludicrous.

A part of me wonders if Pete isn't just happy to have something to pick on me about this morning. After his ordeal last night, getting arrested, all the *fun* he went through, maybe he needed to make someone feel bad, too, instead of letting me try to help him feel better.

But I am fucking fed up. Without looking at him, I say, "I'll be right back."

I walk into our bedroom and into the expansive closet typical of a suburban house like ours, so large to accommodate vast amounts of consumption. Those old houses of the 1920s and '30s had such teeny tiny closets because people back then didn't have hardly any clothes. They had, like, a few items that they hand-washed only and hung to dry, and those little bits probably lasted forever. They're practically still around, aren't they? Men owned, like, one suit, and wore that all year, and maybe owned three or four suits over the course of their lifetimes.

These thoughts about clothes and consumption vaguely haunt the back of my mind as I head to a nook in my side of the closet, where it extends with a low ceiling for extra storage under the stairs. I tuck myself back there and sit, surrounded by Elfa drawers, belts, dresses, and, behind me, luggage and guns in cases. I close my eyes and sit. I imagine a life, a fully realized, happy life—not this sham, not this unhappiness I face here at what I only loosely call "home." I place another circle of blue light around this life (I read that on a spell website someplace) around me and Annie, and as I do, I sit up straighter. I envision a man there (or someone, anyway—I suppose it could be a woman, and I don't really care, a woman might be easier to deal with, I don't know), and then I erase that person. It's just me and Annie, just us, and we are happy. We are happy with what we have and each other, and we accept and we live. A little part of me notices that the person in the other room is removed from this life vision for me. He's not there, and we are happy. I am happier than I have ever been. I just sit, holding this vision. I imagine the feeling I would have every day, the feeling of owning my life, being responsible for whatever it is that I choose to be, and living in my own responsibility. I haven't ever lived like that. I haven't ever even remotely experienced that. I hope it is as great as it sounds. I feel tears deep within my eyes, and my throat has that funny feeling that makes me not able to swallow, just before I cry. It feels blue, too.

I am sure that there is a level of stress that accompanies it, but I bet the reward and feeling of satisfaction for living your own life, living who you want to be at the end of the day, is totally worth it. This person, this future vision of myself— she has it. She knows these feelings, and she lives them. She stands in her own right, and she got there on her own. I see her face; she looks like me. I wish she could tell me how she got there—how I can get there. I sit up straighter. I hold up the blue circle that I have dreamt. Everything is inside it. It is beautiful and complete just the way it is; I don't need or want for anything, content with the love that is right there in that blue embrace.

I hear a baby cry, far away. I start to come back. This isn't the first time I have sat in the closet. I am sure that Pete knows where I am. Sometimes I need to hide, to be in the dark and just sit and sometimes cry.

"Mama." It's Pete's voice. "I think we need you out here."

I reluctantly rise up and go to her. I don't even want to look at him. I feel lost to him. I feel like I have woken up now. I am simply done. I can't talk to him, and I am unable to reveal myself to him in any way. I go to her and only her. I pick her up, and that is where my focus remains. Pete and I do not speak to each other—we talk to Annie. We ignore that elephant following us around our own house, room to room. Pete stays in the bedroom, obviously too tired to deal with a child. I lick my lips. I don't even have to bite my tongue now. I have nothing to say. I just want to be away from him. I want to be gone from him. He doesn't know me. He doesn't know me, and maybe I don't know him. I find that I no longer want to. He can have his God. His guns and country can keep him fucking warm at night.

I take Annie; I feed her; I decide to lay her down for a nap and to take one myself, upstairs in the guest room. I like this room. It's my old bed from the short time after college when I was single, and it feels comfortable and mine. It's an antique from my grandmother, and for some reason I always imagine that my grandfather died on it. I know, yuck, and he didn't, but I was confused when I was little and she told me he died in his sleep. I later found out that he put himself to sleep with a cocktail of pills and booze—put himself to permanent sleep on the sofa. It was his second attempt at permanent sleep. At least, he didn't die in this bed.

My minds drifts as I rest. I think back to a story an acquaintance told me once, about how her husband left her. It was late afternoon on a Saturday in the fall. They were at home, just the two of them. They didn't have children. They were going to watch a movie and have a bite to eat. She got out the DVD of *Bruce Almighty* and was holding it in her hand, ready to put it in the DVD player. She said he just sat there, looking at her, and blurted out, "I'm not happy." She stood, in stunned silence, DVD in hand, in front of the TV, staring back at him. He couldn't look at her anymore. He stood up, picked up his jacket, and left. And that was it. That was just *it*. Well, that was the beginning of the end, anyway.

"I'm not happy." Those words stuck in my head. I liked the clarity and brevity of those words. Of course, I felt for her, and I saw how much it all had hurt her. But with those three little words, she understood. The message could not have been clearer. Was that really how it could go? Could I say that? I felt like I could say it, because it was true.

I fell asleep. The house was silent, with sleeping dogs, sleeping child, sleeping me, all tired for different reasons, all resting off different stresses: Annie learning to put shapes into matching shaped holes; Pete tired from not getting any rest (I assume not getting any rest, anyway) in jail; me tired from getting up at four in the morning; the dogs tired from being dogs and doing dog things, I suppose.

A dank, thick slumber fills the house, and we all sleep. I wake up first, around five o'clock. I can't believe how late it is. I know that Annie has to get up or she won't sleep tonight. God, of course, then the little nagging fear of *Oh god! she's alive, I hope!* fills me. She is; I know she's fine. She probably can sense the stress that fills my moments with Pete. I fully think that children can sense these things and know what's going on, on some level, anyway.

I get her up and head down the stairs, diaper fresh and baby fresh. I think I will spend some money we don't really have and get some dinner, because I don't feel like cooking, not at all. I organize our things. I open the garage with a creak—the door still needs WD-40. *I'll have to fix that or it isn't going to get done*, I think bitterly, and I walk out the door. It opens again right behind me. *Shit*. It's Pete.

"Where are you two off to?"

I barely send a glance his direction. I don't care to look at him. I suppose I should go easier on him, but when has he gone easier on me? Do I turn the other cheek? Not right now. Maybe I'll turn it later. Maybe it is turning, just super-duper slowly. Or maybe I'm just not in the mood.

I catch sight of his face. He looks completely exhausted. His eyes have a puff under their sagging lids, something I have only seen after nights up doing cocaine. Actually . . . hmmm. Who knows on that one, but I wouldn't doubt that there was coke involved last night. Especially since there was anger involved this morning. The bags under his eyes rival the last transatlantic Samsonite I packed. Large. Puffy. Almost painful-looking.

Emotionlessly, I respond. "We're going to get some dinner." I continue what I am doing, loading Annie into her car seat. I lean in and get her buckled. I know that his eyes are following my movements.

"Oh." I can feel his gaze fixed on me. "What's wrong with you?" His tone isn't nasty, and it isn't ugly or demeaning or even demanding. It is just a question.

Nonetheless, I feel the words welling up inside me. I know they are there, dying to get out. They are the only thing in the world that I actually want to say to him—the only words I want to utter in his direction. I don't think about what happens after. I can't escape for good like my friend's ex-husband. I have to come back. I have to return to where I can take care of my baby, to where all her things are and all my things are. We don't have the money to set up shop somewhere else. I am not sure that I have the energy to do that, either.

I think of that person I saw earlier, that future self. I see her smiling in that future world, and I wonder how she got through this moment. She survived it, she did what she had to do to take care of herself, and, in turn, do what she thought she had to do for her daughter. I wonder for a second if she's an actualized witch. I don't even know what that means. Maybe it means a woman in tune with nature and with herself.

I shake that off and swallow, standing, holding my open car door between me and him, feeling the words welling up, ready to come out, like in *Mean Girls*, when she says it's like word vomit, like you can't control the words, they're coming out whether you like it or not, so get a fucking bucket or a raincoat and get ready.

I almost step outside myself. I hear the words come out, I hear them reverberate off the concrete of the garage, and I hear them in the emptiness of the other side or the garage. "I'm not happy." There they are. They are out. And they can't ever be back in.

His countenance immediately reflects exactly what I suspected. He understands. Perfectly. It is crystal clear what I mean. I am not happy in this marriage; I am not happy with you. I know by looking at his expression that he understands, there is no doubt, because he has shifted to full-blown anger in a matter of seconds. I know I could have chosen a better moment, or a better day, for that matter, but I could no longer control it. It had to come out.

I am in my car, on autopilot. I look at him as I reverse out of the driveway. Oh, if looks could kill. He is furious. His eyes have settled into a dead living and fuming look, only made to look more intent by the bags aiding the squint from underneath. He stands there, looking otherwise helpless, in his black Nike shorts and Shady Grove T-shirt and nothing else, stands in the garage, immobile. I can't bear to watch him as I drive away, happy to get away. I flick my eyes to the mirror and see him, watching us drive away. I see him get smaller and smaller. It feels synonymous with the relief I feel, the feeling of getting away from him and making him smaller and smaller to me. Annie is sweetly oblivious to anything. I pray that she doesn't feel or sense anything. I imagine the circle of light protecting her through all of this, and all these things to come.

I drive away and my hands are shaking. I have to go back there. Annie and I go to H-E-B and take our time. We get comfort food. Things like gourmet macaroni and cheese, things like grilled salmon and grilled veggies and chips and sour cream dip, things like containers of soup and wonderful smelling cheeses. I get some wine as well. That sounds like a great idea. I bet Pete and I could both use a drink—in separate rooms, I'd prefer. I move slowly and deliberately through the store. I know that when I get home, I can use my little built-in buffer to avoid anything I need to, at least until she goes to bed. I feel exhausted even imagining what I may have to go through with him. There is nothing I want to say anymore. I just want to be let go. I want it to be easy. I just want him to know that I am no longer happy and I don't think I ever will be, not with you, Pete, and not in this marriage. Not here in suburbia, not on a boat, not with a goat, not anywhere with you. I know, deep down, that I have just started the beginning of the end, that I have set in motion something that cannot be

undone, and I wonder if I was ready. I can't even call Xander
or Gin. It would make it all the more real, and I am not ready
for that. It's already taking on a life of its own, I'm afraid.

We wrap things up here at the store. I get us packed
and loaded into the car, comfort food abundant and me with
no appetite to speak of. I did have a friend tell me about the
divorce diet, that gal who does me a facial every now and
then, and I think, well, there's at least one perk. Not that I
have the least bit of confidence that I can get out of this with
a divorce. I have never entertained that thought seriously,
not in the least. Never have I had the image of myself as a
divorcée. That sounds like something out of a Jackie Collins
novel, not someone thirty-five who has a tattoo and lives in
Austin, Texas.

I turn on the ignition, hear that familiar purr, and set
off toward the house. Dread fills me. Maybe he will have
left. Gone . . . somewhere. To a friend's house? Maybe he'll
have moved out. I know that won't have happened. Wishful,
wishful thinking. I get a text, right at that moment, and it's
from Pete. "Going to the gym." *Thank you, thank you, God,
Goddess, God and Goddess, Nature and Moon and whoever
the fuck I have to thank, Pete, thank you.* I get home to an
empty and clear driveway. I chat with Annie, happy talk to
fill her beautiful and developing mind, and she holds a little
water bottle in her hands, like it is a cherished toy, telling me
about who knows what with her raspy little voice. We chat
and hug and love each other, and I love the purity of that kind
of love and true emotion.

I put everything away and pour a glass of wine for
mama, a sippy cup of milk for her. She eats her macaroni

and cheese, her favorite, "maccy cheese," as she manages to say it. These little, simple acts make me feel good, especially under the sword of Damocles that I know, *know* will fall tonight. I don't text Pete back. I hope that I can be in bed by the time he even gets home. Is that possible? I hope to avoid everything. I don't think that I regret saying it, but I dread the repercussions, especially from him. I sip my wine and sigh, my shoulders fall, and I feel defeated. This, too, shall pass. My phone hasn't rung all day. I should call someone but I don't think I have it in me. I want to sleep—sleep and not wake up until this is all over.

I can't eat. I just drink wine and get Annie down late. I'm taking a bath when I hear him come home, of course, the loud garage door nearly over me as I relax in the tub. I'm scared. I don't want to deal with him or with this. A little part of me wishes that I had never started this ball rolling. But what's done is done. I know that now I have to deal with everything—deal with whatever is going to happen.

I guess a weird part of it is that I don't want to talk. Nothing in me desires speaking, actually talking, to Pete. That could be a problem, I can already see that.

He doesn't come in here. He leaves me alone. I hope that we are just done—done talking for the night, done talking forever. Maybe he'll move out?

I dry off and do all my little product application and toiletry item things that I do after a bath, only I think I am dragging them out slowly, much more slowly than usual, so I can justify going to bed as soon as I am done. I hear the TV blaring from the living room, and I check the monitor as I head for bed. It's barely nine thirty, but that doesn't stop me. I turn out the lights in the bedroom and lay down in bed, sticking close to my side of the bed like a piece of wood, as close to my edge as I can get, light as a feather, stiff as a board, in the darkened room with the monitor beside me. I lie awake, wondering what happens now, but drift off to a fretful sleep, lulled and distracted by the sound of some action movie in the other room.

I notice when Pete slips into bed beside me. We don't touch. We might as well be in a 1950s/'60s TV show, Dick Van Dyke and Mary Tyler Moore or Lucy and Ricky, sleeping in our twin beds. I breathe as quietly as possible and don't move a muscle, hoping not to give away the fact that I am awake. I close my eyes. I want to pray. I want to pray for anything, for help in any way, from anyone, whoever can hear me, so I do. I hope and pray, I pray for strength, I pray for guidance, and I pray to anyone who will listen, to the Moon, to that mysterious God and Goddess, to Mother Nature, to Jesus. I am filled with fear of the future and of what will transpire. I am afraid of the wrath of Pete; that woman I saw, the one who looked like me and seemed so secure in herself, she seems so far away right now. I wish she could be right here to guide me but I can't even really see her, and I wonder if she was just something I made up, just a dream, something that doesn't exist in any universe, parallel or not. I won't allow my body to move, and soon, my fears give way to a deep sleep.

 *Ten*

THE WRONG PRAYERS.

I wake the next morning before Pete and before Annie. That little girl loves her sleep! It's only seven, and the sun is just greeting us. I feel better, less fearful, than I did last night. I hate having an underlying fear that I can't quite identify. It makes a little ball in the pit of my stomach that stays there. I had a friend in college who used to get that, too. We called it "the thing." "I've got the thing," one of us would say to the other, and the other would nod knowingly. There's rarely an easy, identifiable reason for the thing. I've had the thing for a while now, and it won't go all the way away.

I get moving. The monitor is still quiet, so I throw on some workout clothes that I will probably stay in all day, brush my teeth, and pull my hair back from the crazy, curly mess it has dried into overnight into a different crazy, curly mess.

I feel like this situation is easier to avoid during the day. I feel like I can manage it. Annie will be awake; she'll be my buffer. I feel a little guilty using her to block me and Pete from talking, but I am also relieved to have that. The day progresses. Pete gets up and heads to his office, we pass each other, we talk to Annie. He is avoiding it, too. I think he might just give me hateful looks if he acknowledged me, so he is avoiding that. It's just a guess, but that's what I suspect.

The hours drift by and the sun starts to set on an otherwise routine day. I start to feel the dread. Overheard from Pete's office throughout the day were talks with his new lawyer, talks about what happens next about the DUI. I am sure that money was discussed, payment plans, and the like.

Pete comes downstairs when I am feeding Annie dinner. At least I made it nearly twelve hours without having to deal with him.

"So," he says with a long, exasperated sigh, "it looks like this is going to cost in total about six grand. He's thinking that we can get it reduced to a lesser charge so it won't go on my record. He says it's good that I didn't blow and that the video can usually help. The first court date isn't till next week, about my license. So we'll see."

I follow his sigh. "How can we pay for that?" I keep my tone soft and non-accusatory.

"I put it on the USAA MasterCard. I thought then we could at least get the points." He sounds small, defeated. There was a slight hesitation before the word "we."

"OK." I sigh a little sigh again. I should stop that.

Pete slumps off, back upstairs. I call after him. "There's lots to eat here tonight."

I hear a faint acknowledgment of that information from the top of the stairs, something like, "K."

The evening continues like the day did. The focus falls on Annie whenever we are together. I am thrilled but still on eggshells over what will happen the rest of the evening. I continue as I did the night before. I get in bed before Pete; I avoid avoid avoid. I am sitting in bed reading a magazine when he appears in our bedroom doorway.

"Are we gonna talk about this?" he asks.

I put the magazine down and look at him, my eyes wide like a cornered animal. "OK," I reply timidly.

"Do you want me to move out?"

The question. My shoulders slump. Inside me, something is screaming, *Yes!* But I don't have the heart to say that. I have a vision of him in a cheap motel room, like in some movie, with sirens outside and a dirty bedspread, him sitting there, lonesome, probably drunk, and I can't find it within me to answer yes to that question. I exhale loudly and give a little smile at him, tilting my head. "No, I don't think so," I say, in the most noncommittal tone I can muster. I am hoping he will just move out anyway, of his own accord.

"I guess I can just go get an apartment or something."

"We can't even afford that. That's silly. And you wouldn't get to see Annie even." I want him to move out but I am talking him out of it! It's only because I don't want to be the bitch. After all this, when I haven't been the only one who has acted nasty, I can't bear to be the one who essentially kicks him out. I just can't. I want him to not want to be here as much as I don't want him to be here. That sounds way too wishful. I know that in order to get what you want, you have to ask for it. But I can't find it within myself to kick him out of his own house, to tell him I can't be around him. Maybe I could tell him that we just can't talk to each other.

He steps forward into the room, closer to the bed. He is looking more pitiful than ever, puppy dog eyes and all. It's making me sad. Is this the same person who pointed in my face and yelled for me to not open the door, who was making laws in our house, who I feel that I can't be happy with?

I hope that this might be it for the night, and I think I'm right. He doesn't seem to know what to say either. I think he has been stressed all day not only over this, but over that idiotic arrest two nights ago. He pauses as if to say something, but stops. He stops and thinks for a moment, and I sit on the edge of my seat, wondering, what will he say next? Will I be forced to answer a hard question?

I worry about that because I am not in the least a quick thinker when it comes to answering personal questions. I have to have time to mull it over and think about my answer. He can always respond quickly and off the cuff, and keep it convincing, to himself and to others. It's a talent, I think. Whereas I, on the other hand, need lots of time to process the question and get back to you with my prepared answer.

He says, "Maybe we should go to, like, counseling."

I take a deep breath. God, that sounds like about the worst thing I can imagine, but at least there would be another soul there to moderate and hear what I have to endure when he and I have a fight/conversation/discussion. It sounds grueling, awful, horrible, and painful. I still realize that I will have to muddle through it somehow in order to get to the other side, to get to that woman I saw in the future, to cross over to a happier place.

"Yeah. Maybe so." I laugh inside. It's a step. And it avoids anything for now. We can do it there, and we can put it off now. I think he seems relieved, too.

"Do you want me to go sleep upstairs?" he asks sheepishly.

Sheesh! Why do I have to make all the decisions? To be the bitch? Of course I do!

"It doesn't matter," I hear myself reply, afraid to utter what I really want, once again. "Whatever you want to do. You can stay here. Whatever," I repeat, softly.

"OK."

That's what he wanted. I think he might know that I am scared to say what I want, or maybe not? Maybe since he always outright asks for what he wants, he assumes other people do, too. But I can't. I can barely speak to him, much less do something else that will hurt him. I just want it to be over, and I want to escape. I am a fucking poor excuse for anyone standing on her own two feet. Because I don't. Not even close.

I give him a tiny smile, but I make sure it's not a big enough one to arouse any hope—definitely not any hope of getting laid. We are not fucking, no matter how badly I would like sex.

I roll over into my new friend, the wood position, being sure to only occupy the space closest to the edge without rolling off, and I switch off my lamp. That's his cue. This is over for the night, and I am glad.

Days slip by and I have somehow found a counselor—a life coach and therapist that my friend Alexa used when she and her husband, now ex, were splitting after the original "I'm not happy" episode. We have an appointment for later in the week. Of course, it fell on me to hire a sitter and take care of that end of things.

Pete has proceeded to tell his family all about this. His mother called and offered to come up, and she also wants us to come down for church on Sunday, down to San Antonio, to spend family time. I frown when I hear this. Pete thinks it is a great idea and wants us to go, so I have to go. Fuck. What a charade.

We meet with the counselor. His name is Dave, and he looks like a Dave. His office is high in the treetops, blocking what I guess could be an amazing view of downtown, but the trees feel serene, like a treehouse. The office is large and neutral, with touches of warmth here and there. Some family photos decorate his desk, and degrees hang on the wall. We sit over in an arranged sitting area, with a couch in the corner, surrounded by three chairs.

We each meet with him individually, and then he will take us together and try to reconcile our differences, I guess. I debate what to say but decide to spill it. I tell him what I have been up to, that I have done a few little spells, that I have to hide this from Pete, I tell him how stifled I feel, I tell him all of it. He promises confidence. I tell him I don't want to work on this marriage, really, but I feel stifled, I feel like less of a person, and I don't feel like I am with the right person, all of it. I think that I come off as a bitch a little bit, but it has all been pent up for so long that once it all floods out—it ain't pretty.

It's weird because I want Dave to like me. I feel stress about whether he does or not. I feel stress about what he is really thinking about, if he thinks that I am a bad person or a heathen or a bitchy spoiled brat. He gives me worksheets called "Lifestyle Management." It's a twenty-three page honker of a thing designed, as the tagline at the bottom of the front page makes it clear, to be "a program for taking full responsibility for your personal success and happiness." I like that part of it. I think it's really to help me sort out my life, to help me figure out exactly how it is that I want to live and what I want. I think he senses that I just don't know right now, and that I might have lost myself somehow. Or maybe I was never even found to begin with.

I leave, and Pete goes in. Finally, I am called in to all discuss together. I sat in a chair before but now Pete is on the sofa, so I reluctantly sit by him. Luckily, I don't get asked too many of the questions. Our counselor, Dave, does most of the talking. He talks about our communication and how we can listen to each other. I pay close attention. I want to use his tips. I want to become a better communicator. Our communication is broken, and I don't know how to fix it, not at all.

He gives us sheets with arrows and little flow charts and lots of words. I wonder about Dave's communication skills a little bit. But I hope that Pete is listening, too, and getting something out of it. It feels complicated and confusing, thinking about all that goes into this flow chart and everything. It's all about situation and impact and response and results, and he talks about making these skills into habits. My brain doesn't do well with complicated issues. I do hope, however, that we can communicate together. I feel that faint hope once again. It feels familiar. What also feels familiar is the lack of belief I have in it. But maybe these tips will be useful, even if we have to use the skills through a divorce. Dave uses a lot of business models, I think because he specializes more in business and job therapy. He encourages us to think of our partner as a "customer." That's weird. But whatever, if it means better communication, I guess I'll try it.

Dave also asks us to do an online quiz about relationship satisfaction. He also recommends that we read M. Scott Peck's *The Road Less Traveled*. Then we will bring it all in next week for comparison.

We leave, and I want to make time to do all my worksheets. They look good. They are all about figuring out exactly how we really want to live our lives. I love a nice worksheet, especially if I get to make a list or two. Plus, I know that when I feel jealous of someone or something, it means I really need to be living that, whatever it is, like when I talk with Gin. It's not about material things. It's about people who practice yoga, or people who drive hybrids or eat organic or cook a lot. Or become witches.

I think Pete and I both feel strangely optimistic, for different reasons. We didn't really communicate at all during the session, but we feel like we got something accomplished anyway.

I find myself taking these things I was told to do very seriously. I think it's because I am really interested in redesigning my life. I love that idea, and I love this assignment. Looking toward what I really want resonates with me. I realize that I have a deep dissatisfaction with how I have currently designed it, which I was involved in doing, despite how much I would like to believe otherwise.

I talk to Xander that day, I tell him what's been happening. He is like, "Oh my god, what the fuck happened?" totally shocked, but then he starts to come around as we talk. He ends up saying something that sticks with me, ticks in my head. "You know, V, it actually seems like you've been playing along for a very long time."

Later that night, I take the relationship satisfaction test. It's super long. It has over a hundred questions, and they require thought. But hey, it keeps Pete and me separately occupied, and that, to me, is a fine thing. I appear to be working on our relationship when in actuality I think I am avoiding working on it.

So this quiz ranks all different aspects of the relationship, from feeling appreciated and loved, to love for partner, to sex life, to security, to meeting the need to communicate. It then produces my score and gives a ranking from one to one hundred for each category. I score low on just about everything. My highest ranks are support and security at 68, financial issues at 67 (did I answer those right?), and parenting issues, also at 67. It goes into great detail breaking down what each thing means with an extensive paragraph. I have a tie for the lowest score: I got a 25 each for meeting the need to communicate and spending time together. Not surprising there. Everything else ranked in the thirties and forties, just about. Sex life scored an impressive 55, even though there hasn't been any to speak of, at least none together, in over a month, and there's none on the horizon. I wonder how low things would be if this quiz was put on a curve and that was the basis. And how in the hell did financial issues score higher than sex? Wow. Things must be really bad. Apparently, I am incredibly dissatisfied.

At the end of the quiz is a little bullet pointed page that gives you things to watch out for and things that need work. Our quality time together needs work. Um, ya think? The word "rut" leaps to mind.

Pete hasn't done his yet. He has been working the rest of the day, and he keeps it up the next day, too. Or rather, "working." He worked out, he did all the things he needed to do, he acknowledged Annie briefly, he kept moving at his usual frantic pace. Annie and I sat and watched the whirlwind go by, peaceful and at home, getting out when we could. I have been appreciating Austin all I can, appreciating all the beautiful people who live life on their own terms, those people who live however they want, take care of themselves and their children as they see fit, live their own lives that I find myself admiring more and more every time I catch sight of one of them.

I feel the twinge of jealousy. I look around and see people being real to themselves and living on their own terms, and I know that's what I want. I want to be on my own, taking care of Annie. I don't want a dissatisfying marriage. I don't want to work on something like this that I would rather send to the scrap heap because I can't feel what I am supposed to feel. I can't seem to get there or muster anything of the sort. I wish it would just magically happen. But I know that the words have to come from me, out of my mouth. Getting them out seems impossible still. Why am I so scared still? What am I afraid of?

Sunday arrives without incident, I guess. Unless you consider not talking to each other at all and not having any kind of real marriage an incident. It's an anti-incident.

I have been dreading this day. I even flipped through my good spell book, looking for something that might relieve me of having to go to church with his family, to no help at all. Then I tucked it back into its hiding place. I just mainly sat around and wished for it all to go away.

I got up and got Annie looking as cute as possible, since I am pretty sure that families often measure how good of a mom you are by how cute and well groomed your child appears. So Annie is in a dress, with tights, bows in her hair, the whole nine.

I, however, am another story. Hopefully Pete has not told his family too much. I make the best effort I can to tame my mane and find something that doesn't look slutty, or only looks a teensy bit slutty and only if you're looking, because hey, it's hard for a girl to let go of her roots. I dress all in black: black pants that fit well, a tucked-in fitted black button-down shirt, and a long necklace that Xander made. Heels. This will do.

We make it out fifteen minutes past schedule because Pete had to fuck around in the garage this morning for some reason. He is rushing around, asking me to do things for him, "Can you iron my shirt?" What the fuck, I hate to iron. I do it anyway, all the while thinking, *I won't miss this.*

We leave in a flurry, in my car, Pete driving like crazy and calling them with a lie, straight up, "Sorry, Annie had a bad diaper at the last minute, it was a mess!" A wasted lie. Sometimes I figure we may only have so many lies we can get away with in one lifetime, so why waste them on stupid little shit?

We make it to San Antonio in record time. I bet Pete has made it faster, though. We arrive at church and head inside. Pete gets Annie out while I grab some gum. He's composing himself, and mass has already begun. His parents have been watching for us. They have saved us seats.

His mother is like a nun in that she is so sweet in appearance that you'd want to confess to her and have her feed you communion and be your mother, no matter who you are. The story goes that once she wanted to be a nun, too. Her name is even Mary. Mary is so good to me, never a harsh word, always there and kind and loving—a great mom and grandma, too. I see her soft gray hair, cut in a little round bob, peeping up from the pew as Pete's dad Dick waves us over, eagle eye that he is. We traipse over to the pew, through the standing-room-only crowd, and I am sure that saving these seats was not an easy task.

We say quiet hellos to everyone. I see that his brother John, his wife Abby, and their two children, Aidan and Holden, are there, too. The whole family is here. Probably to rally behind us as we face marital strife. An internal *ugh* envelops me.

Mass continues, and I have officially zoned out. Annie is being good, only fussed a little once, and Pete was the lucky one who stepped into the back with her. She's not quite to that age where she's trouble in church just yet, even though I look forward to that day because it means I can leave, too.

It's time for communion, the Eucharist. We all head up there in a line, Pete clutching Annie, and I tuck my gum on a back tooth and take communion, too. I like this part, for some reason. I like the wine, and I like what it all symbolizes. I chew up my wafer, and my gum gets loose. A little bit of the wafer gets caught in my gum and this makes me laugh, because I have Jesus caught in my gum. I laugh and grab Pete's arm, leaning toward him as we walk, and I laugh under my breath, and I whisper, "I got some stuck in my gum."

Pete rounds on me. He turns and frowns, but tries to keep up appearances. "What? Then you need to swallow it," he replies, in total seriousness.

I frown back, my laughter gone. "No!" I whisper yell back at him. It was just a little funny. I really doubt that Jesus and God give a rat's ass whether a little wafer gets in my gum or not, and if they do, then they need to start focusing on more important issues, right away.

I drop it, and so does he. We keep up an appearance for his parents, their priest, their friends, his brother. We make it through the rest of the service and head out to the car for a home-cooked meal at his parents' house. I am getting used to this feeling of dread, this knot in the pit of my stomach.

As we walk to the car, Pete says, "You aren't supposed to chew gum in church. You still need to swallow that."

I cannot believe that he is still thinking about this, still on this! "What, did you learn that in Catholic school?"

"Yes, and you aren't supposed to."

"They told the kids that so they wouldn't chew gum during mass. That's what that was about." I am really still stunned that we are even still discussing this.

"No, V, it's disrespectful and just wrong."

"I cannot believe that we are still discussing this." I turn my head and pull a Julia Roberts in *Pretty Woman*, blowing my gum hard out of my mouth and into the grass nearby. "There. Now a bird can have some forgiveness."

He looks at me, mad, and huffs out of his nose. "You are unbelievable." He drags out that words so it sounds like three separate words. Un. Be. Lievable.

"So are you, frankly," I retort, frowning and nodding. I know deep down that there is no way I can make it with someone who didn't find any humor at all in Jesus in my gum.

We get in and drive the short distance to his parents' house in North San Antonio, near the military base where his father was stationed until his retirement ten years ago. The house is a throwback to the Brady Bunch era, but not quite. If you ask me, there is a certain sweetness to a house that isn't old enough to be cool but not new enough to be new. It has the mix of stone, brick, and wood all along the outside. The wood looks fresh but is a stale green color. The yard is always immaculate and trimmed to perfection. Inside, there have been updates throughout the downstairs, and it is lighter and airier than I imagine it was in years past.

Abby pulls me aside as we walk in the door, into the stiff and stuffy dining room, which looks like it is trying to be regal and classic but is small, dated, and I find to be exceptionally unrelaxing for a meal. I back into a tall wooden chair that's been lemon-Pledged within an inch of its life.

"Hi!" I say, not having seen her since Annie's first birthday six months ago.

"Hi!" she replies, terminally perky. "Listen, I know it's

a little weird since we all know what's going on," she says, not knowing that is news to me, yet she continues, "but I wanted you to know that we have all been through it. That's just what happens dealing with these Cantrell men! I mean, John and I went through a time when I didn't think I would ever even be able to stand being with him. I couldn't even look at his face, it would make me so mad. And then we went to counseling and it was like, once you open those floodgates, out pours all kinds of stuff, just all coming out."

There is a certain wisdom to what she is saying. She goes on as I nod.

"I would be in my car driving and just want to keep driving and never go home," she confides in a near whisper. She tugs on the edge of her cardigan, which is peppered with multicolored polka dots the size of ping-pong balls. "Then, we came out the other side—we made it through. Now, he is my soul mate. I can't imagine life without him. It can get so much better, I promise you. Once I started taking Lexapro, that made all the difference to me, too. So much of it can be hormonal, especially after having a child."

Oh my god. Wait. Am I really hearing this? I nod, not knowing what to say. Maybe I should say congratulations?

"I just wanted to tell you that you can get through it. We have all been there, and we all got through it. I didn't want you to feel weird about today or anything."

Way to accomplish that, girl. I know she means well.

I feel super weird, but I don't say so. I thank her instead. I know that she is trying to help, that they all are in their own odd ways. I decide to keep my trap shut and not say anything about me and Pete. I have a feeling that she will hear enough over time, and I don't really need to add fuel to this fire.

We then move through the kitchen and into the breakfast room, where everyone is talking and the table is set for us to all sit together and have a family meal. Things are cooking in the kitchen, and I am down with this; I usually love Mary's home cooking. Wine is being poured, and I am thankful that they drink. Of course, Pete already has a beer in his hand so it looks like I will be driving, especially since he doesn't quite exactly have a license anymore even though he drove down here. The last thing he needs to do is drive after a couple cold ones. I keep an eye on Annie, who has wandered out the double doors attached to the breakfast room and is looking for the cat, a fat orange tabby named Molly that she is forever lusting after petting. Of course, Molly wants nothing to do with her.

We all mill around. I still keep my mouth shut, probably too shut; I bet they would like me to open up a little. Actually, on second thought, that isn't true, I bet; they probably think they want to know but then wouldn't, really—like when you are so curious about what someone is going through but then once they start to spill it, you go, "No, no, I don't think that I want to know any of this. Can I hit rewind?" Sometimes, what's worse is that it's boring. My stories aren't even that dramatic; they're just stories. They would be from my personal perspective anyway, and whose side do I think these people are really going to take anyway? Their son/brother/ brother-in-law or a wannabe witch who attempts spells and takes their grandchild to a store with a pentacle hanging on the wall?

The standing around and the busywork continues for what seems like an eternity. I spy Pete opening another beer. Maybe his third? I'm not sure. Watchdog me, counting drinks consumed so I know what version of him I will be dealing with. Finally we sit down to eat, after I have done woman's work: helping with the cooking, laying out the butter, lighting the candles on the table, and generally keeping my hands busy while we all avoid the subject of marital strife, a trend I hope will continue. I can't imagine that it's going to come up at the Sunday lunch table, like, "Oh, I hear you guys have started marriage counseling?" "Oh, yeah! Have you tried it? It's really interesting, and we are learning so much!"

We sit down and all hold hands for the blessing, a tradition in their house. Annie is in a high chair next to me. She tries to recite the blessing right along with Pete's dad, throwing in little nonsense words here and there that I am sure make sense to her. We all say amen. I push her little brown curls off her forehead and tighten her two pigtails, fixing her plate and getting her all set to eat.

There is talk at the table of how beautiful everything looks and smells, with oohs and aahs over Mary's cooking: a beef brisket, salad, mashed potatoes (that I totally have my eye on), bread and butter, and a bowl of fruit. It's all so well-balanced and perfect. I never make meals like this. It doesn't really ever occur to me to put bread and butter on the table with a meal. Cindy Crawford used to say that bread makes your butt big. The women here have larger than average butts, that is true, so maybe there is something to that. But I am ready to pack some down and enlarge my own ass right this minute. I take it all, am thrilled at the prospect of the potatoes, and don't skimp.

There is small chit-chat over the table: pass this, and could you hand me that? Little things said. I am feeling better; it is truly a wonder what a couple of bites of potatoes can do for the mind and soul.

Pete passes the brisket, and I open my mouth. "Thanks for making all this, Mary! It looks great." I try to keep it sweet but understated. "I never make meals like this. It's so nice."

Pete pipes up. "No, you don't!" He laughs his "I'm only joking, aren't I funny?" laugh while he says this and looks around. "You want to take these candles home though?"

Abby's curiosity is aroused. "What does that mean? Do you like them?"

"Oh, he's just," I wave my left hand in the air, like I am swatting at an invisible fly, probably a subconscious attempt at shooing away this line of talk. "He's just giving me a hard time cause I like candles."

Pete does a kind of harrumph at this notion, that I like candles, and he can't keep his mouth shut. He takes a swig of his beer. "She likes 'em, all right. She wants to light them up and cast spells around them." He holds his hands to each side, dramatically, but still a small movement, like he's reading a crystal ball.

They all look at me. I look at my food, then at Pete. I am really unsure of what to say now. I glance at Mary's face, and there is a faint look of alarm there. I see Abby look to John, and then down at her plate. There is some shifting in seats. I hear breathing. Is it my own? I suppress the hatred I am feeling for Pete at the moment. I stay calm and what I think is cool, although sometimes how you perceive you are behaving and the way it comes across are two drastically different things. I try to keep them as together as possible.

I decide to tell the truth in hyperbole, to make a joke of it, so maybe no one will know that it is the somewhat the truth. This may not be the best approach but it might change the subject. "Yeah, right," I say, "I'm sitting around with a bunch of candles casting spells. For what? I think I'd cast a spell for the house to get clean, the dishes to get done without me."

I chuckle and I hope that this lightened the mood. I shoot Pete a look, a look that says, "Shut up because you are saying too much and I am feeling weird so just save it." And he doesn't even give a shit. I know he doesn't give a shit because he opens his mouth again.

"No," he laughs, his attempt at keeping this light, like it is all funny to him, "You cast spells for Xander to get him money and for who knows what else. You've looked up all kinds of stuff on your computer. I've seen it."

Oh, there it is. He's been looking over my shoulder on my computer. Not literally, but big-brothering me, clearly.

I blush and reach to pull on my earlobe but trying to keep my chin up right now. This family is way too Catholic for this. They might hold me over the chiminea outside after lunch if they suspect I am a witch. Which I am not! I would be about the poorest excuse for a witch, ever. I am simply trying to figure out what a witch is to me, what it would mean to me, and if I want to be one, that's all.

"OK, you're totally exaggerating." I am staring down at the brisket and glancing at Pete every second or so. "And I'm just curious and looking at stuff on my computer, it's not a big deal. There are lots of people that look at worse stuff than that on their computers."

John clears his throat. Mary is still quiet, and Abby looks officially uncomfortable.

Abby tries to calm things after her question helped get this ball rolling. She goes with my subject change, remarking, "Oh, I have to really watch the boys—we keep all kinds of controls over our computers at home but I know they have friends. When they go to their houses, they look at who knows what!"

I give her a grateful look and a small smile. I also think, *I bet she has no idea the things they can look at on the internet.* Aidan is still upstairs playing video games and hasn't even bothered to come down to eat, not that anyone really misses the company of a fourteen-year-old very much. But I would actually welcome a fourteen-year-old at this moment. And as far as the internet and its contents go, I barely even have an idea, but I do know that it can be shocking, even to my exposed and tolerant and witchesque self.

How will Pete respond? I don't think that I can say anything without inciting some sort of anger from him, not now, a week after his DWI. Maybe I should play dirty and throw that in. But Pete drops it. He doesn't say anything.

I can't even look at him. I know that his reaction was my cue to keep my mouth shut, not to say anything at all. But I feel like exploding. I know that Mary and Pete's dad are probably still thinking about what he said, Mary especially. I bet she hates the idea of her son being around a woman checking out spells and interested in what she would probably label "dark arts." OK, that's from Harry Potter, but still,

I think that they would think of it that way. I wish I was a better articulator because I would stand up here and try to explain or defend myself, and all of a sudden I push my chair back and stand up.

I feel like I am suddenly stepping outside of myself. This isn't something that I would ever normally do. But I have a moment, a moment of, what have I got to lose? These people? Not my daughter, certainly not her, I know that much. If all the crazy celebrities can retain custody then I most certainly can, too. So I now find myself standing up, physically and metaphorically, and looking down at everyone. Annie's clueless face is there to support me, love me, not caring what I say, as long as I am there to love her, the one person at this table who is not judging me.

"You know what, Pete? I am a good and lovable woman, and if you don't love me the way I am, interested in more than being Catholic and interested in studying spirituality—" I see him scoff at that, and I call him out. "Don't scoff, because that is exactly what it is. I want to live in a home where I am free to do whatever it is that I want to do, even if it's answering the door or reading about nature and spells and whatever else—"

Pete interrupts, standing up, too, asserting his five inches of height on me, puffing up like a bird. "No, no, everyone here knows that you made a promise when we got married, a promise to raise our children Catholic and—" (out comes the finger) "—this completely goes against that. It goes against your promise."

Dick stands up too, now. "Let's all just sit down, now, and this is something the two of you can discuss together when you go to the, um—" (I know the word is practically foreign to him) "—um, counselor, right, so let's just sit on down and eat and have a nice meal."

Sorry, Dick, I think we've blown that.

Mary chimes in, seconding Dick. "Peter," she always calls him by his full name, "Peter, just sit, and Veronica, you, too. Why don't we say a little prayer over this, that all our hearts are healed through all of this?"

Actually, I think that is a sweet idea. While I am not up for praying right now, necessarily, I get what she is doing. I think, *OK, maybe we can pray to someone for some strength and tolerance and understanding.* Dick, Pete, and I all sit back down and she begins, grabbing Dick's hand and John's hand, trying to get the hand holding going. I am sitting between Annie and Pete, and there is no way on God's green earth that I am holding Pete's hand right now, so I only take Annie's, half of me dreading what Mary is about to say, but waiting to see.

"Dearest heavenly Father, we pray to you, we pray to you, Mary, and to you, Jesus, the Holy Spirit."

Is that the superfecta? I wonder, as she continues.

"We pray that you heal this marriage, this beautiful union that you oversee, that you keep watch over these two wonderful souls you have created in your sight and consecrated in your name. We pray that you just lift them up and show them how you are there every moment of every day, blessing them and caring for them."

I start to rub my forehead with my free hand. I take a deep breath, searching for something that I can agree with in this prayer. Blessings, OK, that one is true enough, I know that, as I hold Annie's beautiful little baby hand, small and perfect and warm and soft.

"We pray that you give this perfect union a strength that comes out on the other side. You know exactly what you are doing here, and you have a perfect plan in your sight, so we pray that you keep and hold these two through this time and make them so much stronger through it. In his name we pray, Our father . . ."

And they are off saying the Lord's Prayer. I don't feel like it, so I am quiet, sitting through this episode and aching to get out, to escape with, with what intact, exactly? And what did I agree with there?

"Kingdom come, thy will be done . . ." they all chant, together.

Maybe this is kind of like a spell—a collective drawing on like-minded souls for a common goal. It's not that much different. The problem here is, I don't want this. Strengthening a bond with this person sounds like misery. I don't want to be bound to anyone who would treat me this way.

I know that the family means well. It's just that this is about the last thing I feel like doing. I already went to church today, for god's sake. (Or goddess's. Whoever.)

"Amen." Finally.

Everyone goes back to their lunch. All is quiet. I guess that did it. That silenced us. But I realize that I was interrupted. I didn't even get to finish what I was saying when I stood up! *Maybe that is for the best*, I think. Maybe it is good that I wasn't allowed to continue. I cannot wait to get out of here. But then, of course, I will be trapped in a car with Pete for an hour.

Thank goodness Annie naps. I stress that we should go when she can sleep in the car, so we head out right after lunch. We all say our goodbyes, and the family, everyone but Aidan, anyway, who is still inside playing video games, walks us all the way out to the car to bid us farewell, just like they always do. We all hug multiple times and there are multiple goodbyes, but both Mary and Abby feel it necessary to whisper things in my ear as we part.

Abby goes first. As we hug and I say a quick bye, knowing something is coming, she hugs me and says softly, "Remember what I told you. This is just what we have to deal with in these Cantrell men. And you might think about getting your hormone levels checked. Things can get all messed up and crazy after a baby," she adds with a smile.

I stifle a cringe and manage to nod my head, pulling away. I am a little insulted about the hormone business because who is to say that even if my hormones were crazy, I wouldn't still be right? It's like teenagers, everything is blamed on raging hormones, as if they can't just also be making decisions.

I hug John for the second time, then Dick. Mary has saved me for the very end. She pulls me close as we hug and says a prayer in my ear. I am facing the car and Pete, and he is staring at us. I find myself giving a blank stare to the hood of the car, as I listen to her prayer for me and for Pete, to send us on our way.

"Heavenly Father, I lift these two up to you and just ask for healing with the two of them. I pray over this daughter of mine—" (meaning me) "—that she can rise up and do what is necessary to save this marriage, consecrated and blessed in your name and in your sight, and for the sake of that beautiful little creation of yours, that they may have a wonderful life *together*—" (lots of stress on that word!) "—through you and in you. In Jesus' name, Amen."

She looks at me lovingly and a half-smile crosses my lips. Not exactly the prayer that I would have said, but she was sweet and trying, I guess. She loads me into the driver's seat and then walks around to Pete's side. She has already said goodbye to him but he rolls down the passenger side window. She bends down, peeping inside, and says another goodbye.

"Goodbye, you two." She gives that a second thought. "You three!" Then a switch to seriousness with a side of sugar. "Now, you two," she adds gently, "be sure to pray together. That makes all the difference in a marriage." I start the engine. "You must take the time, every day, to pray together." I put it in drive, not to be rude, but it's as if I can't control it, my body is doing things to get out of here. She smiles, relieved that she has given us that key to marital happiness. "God bless you."

I internally *ugh*, even though I know that this is spiritual and all well-meaning. I internally cringe again at a vision I have of me and Pete, sitting together in front of the fireplace, hands clasped, him praying. Oh, no. I want to wipe this image from my mind. It sounds awful to me, and I wonder if there are married couples everywhere who are doing this and saving their marriages. I feel Pete looking at me, and I glance over. We make eye contact for a second. His expression is blank and unreadable. It doesn't say love or sorry or contempt or anything; it's just blank. I look quickly back to the road, and we drive, in silence, back to Austin, Annie dozing delicately in the back.

 *Eleven*

I WANT TO GO THROUGH NEW MOTIONS.

We get home and go through the motions, again and again, the same thing—that's all our lives consist of anymore I feel like. I am boring; I just do these things. If you add in going to church and praying together, I don't know if I can take it. I might explode or go insane.

I feel an insatiable need to get out or to get Pete out. What am I waiting for? What? I wish I knew. I just feel . . . scared. Like I have to *grow up*. I am scared to do it. I think that maybe I should take Annie and go. I wonder about this, and I seriously, to my surprise and mild horror, start to entertain the thought. If I am going to go through the motions, then I need them to be new motions. I need them to be all new to me and unexpected and *something*. Maybe it's having a child that does this. While there is so much new to discover with this amazing little person, I also think that there is a rut factor that encroaches because of the scheduling it requires and the change that it can put on the parent's life. And that's what I feel. I need new motions to go through. I need a plan.

So I think that I will consult my little spell book late tonight, just to see what it says about finding a new path, or something of that sort. Is this stalling? No, surely not. It's part of *the plan*. I *think*. We go to bed, and I use the excuse of a little sound from Annie floating across the monitor to go up and "check" on her. I slip into the closet first and grab my book, secretly stashed in my box with the sexiest shoes I own—some Guiseppe Zanotti heels that come up around my ankle, that are practically too painful to wear, but they're crazy hot and I got them 75% off.

I creep out of the bedroom, hiding my book and feeling relatively safe that Pete is sleeping. Not that I care that much anymore. *Let him find me*, I riskily think. *Let him see me reading this book of good spells, and let this be the final straw.* Of course, I know from not long ago to be careful what I wish for. But the feeling of not caring is becoming too strong.

My feet pad up the stairs. I retreat into the guest room, where I turn on the light and curl up in the big, overstuffed mossy brown chenille chair in the corner, ready to do something. I read and read and try to find something, anything, that falls into a change of circumstance spell that I can modify to use right now, no candles, no nothing, just me and the night and the waning moon and my book. I flip through, laughing as I encounter one spell designed to bring the love of a mother-in-law. I settle on combining two spells: one for getting another to agree, and one to make a wish come true. There are candles involved in both, but I don't worry about that. I get up and rifle around, digging up a pen and a scrap of paper torn from an old Mad Libs that I keep in the nightstand up here. I think hard about my wish. Finally, I write:

I wish to stand on my own as a woman and as a mother, and I wish for true happiness, even though I don't even know what that really means. Show me. Help me. Please.

I turn out the light and sit in the glow of the moon pouring in the window. My heart dwells on this thought. I don't let it go and don't try to define it. I just sit with it for what feels like a long time. I then take it and tear it up into tiny bits. I was supposed to burn it in the candle, but I figure this is good enough. I turn the light back on and consult my book, ready to say the little incantation to get another to agree. I would like Pete to let me be—to agree to let me be what I want to be and live however I want to live.

I start to say the incantation in a voice lower than a whisper, keeping the light on in the room this time. "Please, Pete, do think again. May the consequence heal my pain. Grant my request to me, and you'll see, the good in your heart will set me free. Bless you." I have a flash to this afternoon, when Mary said "God bless" to us both, or rather us three, and I know that she meant it. I am not sure who I am asking to bless him at this moment, but I go with it anyway, figuring that the force in the universe and all that is good will hear and go with it.

I think I hear a faint creak or a noise behind me, but I ignore it, sure that it is just a house or a wind noise. I start to whisper the incantation again, my voice barely audible even to me, when suddenly, the door opens, and in struts Pete. He has fire in his eyes.

"What are you doing?" he asks angrily, accusatory, as if he has caught me with my coven, dancing naked under the moonlight.

I play it cool. "Just sitting here, thinking." I have a frown on my face, making it apparent that I do not like his tone or his near accusation.

He firmly stomps over to where I sit facing the window, my legs casually tossed over one of the chair arms so I can see the moon outside, that waning moon partially blocked by the clouds. Pete snatches the book from my hands, even though I had it shut and the hard red cover was all that was showing, looking innocuous.

"What the fuck is this?"

"You know what, Pete? You could actually try to talk to me like a normal person."

"You know what, Veronica? I would, if this was at all something that a normal person would do. After all that today, here I find you sitting here hiding and doing spells in the middle of the night. No, not normal." Cue his incredulous laugh. "Not normal at all!"

I feel a calm wash over me, probably inspired by the fact that I just don't really care anymore. I take a nice, deep breath and sigh it out, loudly. I nod and scratch my head. Blankly, I look and him, and I say what I am thinking. I just say it, for a change. "I'm done." I shake my head. "I'm just done." I look out the window. I open my mouth to say something else, but Pete jumps in.

"Oh, good! Good! That is such a mature and adult attitude. Just declaring that you're 'done.' Well V, it isn't that simple. We have a lot of things we need to get through here, and your immaturity is not helping. All you are doing is being completely selfish and immature."

I get up and take the book out of his hand, pulling hard on it and meeting his eyes in defiance. It feels like there is some parent and child situation going on here, like some kind of roles we are acting out. Maybe I am falling into the child, but it's hard not to when he is trying to act like a restrictive father. I wonder, *Am I being immature? Is this selfish, to want to read and do what I want to do?*

"Pete, isn't it truly selfish to want someone else to live the way you tell them to?" I keep my voice calm.

He exhales loudly through both nostrils, practically snorting. "No, V, you agreed to this. You made the promise to raise our daughter the way we discussed. You made these decisions and promises and now don't want to keep them. You just want to go off and cast spells and be a witch, I guess." He gives a shake of his head and jerky shrug. "You agreed to this, and now, when it comes time to do it, you want to run away. You're just running away."

I feel more like he is determined to think these things, so I just let him. And maybe he is right. Maybe I do want to run away, and maybe it is immature. But what I do know is that I cannot and will not live this life anymore. If I want to read something, then I am fucking going to read it. If I want to do something and it doesn't hurt anyone else, then what's all the fuss about? Aren't we all entitled to our own versions of spirituality? Or is it that once we say, "OK, this is what I believe," then that's it, we are stuck with that forever? No. No, no, just, *no*.

I brush past Pete and head down the stairs, with him following close behind me. I hear him breathing from getting all worked up. While I wonder if he is right about me, I also wonder if he isn't the exact same way. I wonder if his maturity level is all that high, when he can't even handle it and talk to me and try to find out what it is that I really believe. That has never even been discussed here, and I would like for it to. I am not having an affair, and I am not being a bad person, but I can't live a double life, not at all. I make it to our bedroom before he does. I close the door and lock it behind me. He immediately tries the knob, to find it locked. I don't want any more of this. I had the presence of mind to bring the baby monitor, thank God, and I hear Pete, fully irate, on the other side of the door.

"Thanks for just proving my point, Veronica. Really mature. Fine. If this is the way you want it."

I wait, hoping that the next sentence will bring something huge, like "I'm moving out," or "Let's get a divorce," or something, anything, but instead, he says, "That's fine, I'll just sleep on the couch."

And with that, I hear the TV turn on. I sit down on the edge of the bed, feeling tears welling up in my eyes.

 *Twelve*

EVEN SAINTS AND WITCHES HAVE OFF MOMENTS.

I wake up the next morning with tears crusted in my eyes, knowing that this is over and I am not living like this. The time has come.

My brother called me and woke me, obviously having had spoken to someone. He told me that working on this marriage could take eighteen to twenty-four months, like it's a scientific formula. And I was like, "Oh, OK, yeah, sure, thanks," not telling him what I really thought, which was, *Are you fucking kidding me? Going through nearly two years of work on this does not sound worth it, especially when there is no guarantee on the other side.*

He continues and tells me, "You have to try." He goes on, and I listen, as he tells me how divorce is wrong and if we split up it will be detrimental to Annie. I was fully and easily reminded why we don't talk all that often. Then he started in about my spirituality, about how I have strayed from the Lord, and how the Lord wants me to come back. He wanted to pray with me. I wanted to hang up. But then I thought, *There I go, being immature again, I suppose*, giving Pete cause and reason and justification. We finally ended that call. He insisted that I just think about things, and I agreed, but it was a lie. My mind is made up and isn't changing. I want out. I cannot stay with this person who refuses to change or allow change from me.

I get out of bed and go wash my face, sticking with cold water to wake up, and brace myself for what must be done. I have no idea how I will have money. I will go to work and figure out something, but for now, I can stay with Xander and so will Annie. She will go with me.

Pressing my ear against the monitor, I don't hear a thing. I guess she is still asleep. I am up really early; my brother must have called at six on the dot. Weird. And how could it possibly get worse? That is never a good question to ask. I pack, furiously, knowing that there will probably be a scene attached to this leaving I am going to do, but I do know that he won't be willing to take care of Annie. That just isn't even in the realm of possibility anyway.

I have a moment of fear fill me. I grab the monitor and press my ear against it again, listening intently for any sign of breathing, fearful that Pete has taken Annie during the night and left with her. There isn't anything that scares me more. I listen and listen, and finally, I hear a tiny baby sigh and movement. I sit down, feeling the tension fall from my forehead and shoulders and neck, noticing that my shoulders must have been fully up to my ears.

I get stuff packed and have no idea if I have what I need, as I am not in my right mind to be packing for anything at the moment. I cannot think straight. But I know that I can come back and get what I need. I think, *I should grab some files, tax files, house papers, stuff like that, my passport,* and I prepare to open the door and go upstairs. But necessities like baby gear and toothbrushes take precedence.

Pete is passed out on the sofa, phone next to him, TV still on, muted. I guess he was talking to people late last night and I didn't hear him for the sound of the TV.

The wheels of my suitcase are very loud on the tile so I pick it up and set it by the door. I dash upstairs and root through files, grabbing the ones I might need, planning to make copies of them—our home closing statements, anything that involves money, my statements, my documents, Annie's documents, stuff like that. I need my computer, too.

I go back down and shove the files in the bag, hoping that I won't wake him. I grab my computer, too, and open the garage door as quietly as possible, wishing that I had taken the time to WD-40 that squeak. It doesn't rouse him, and for that I shoot a little whispered thank you to whoever is watching over me.

But at the same time, I hope he wakes up. Let there be a scene. I feel braver than I have throughout this whole thing. I feel ready to stand up. I feel like I am moving forward, and it feels right. I know that he can bring me down and put me down, but I can still keep going, worrying about how to get those words out of my head later. I know it will end, because everything does, eventually.

I make it out the door and get the bag in the car. Now I'm heading up to pack Annie. I don't care if we have to sit at IHOP for three hours until Xander wakes up and answers his phone, I'll do it. With that thought, I reach into the pocket of my black sweats and grab my phone, sending him a text that I am sure will blow his mind. But of course, he knew that I had to do the whole church thing yesterday and is probably fully prepared for that not to have gone well. So I text him, silently typing: *Taking Annie and moving out. Don't call, will call you later. We are coming to your house. Thx honey.*

And I feel thankful, fully grateful, that we have somewhere to go.

Sometimes I think about the women who are abused, who endure day after day of physical or verbal torture, and I think that it is no wonder that they don't leave. Even with this little bit that I have been exposed to, I notice that it is often all that sticks in my head. I go over and over those things that I have been told—that I am a bad mother, that I am selfish, immature, all those nasty things that Pete has said, and all the nasty ways that he has said them—and I think that there must be some truth in them. Otherwise, why would he say them? But what about all those women, all those souls who don't deserve a bit of the untruths that they are told? Their self-worth must be down in the negative numbers. It makes me so sad. It makes me wonder what is true and what is not. It also makes me know that I will not let this break my spirit.

I can't worry about all that right this minute. I roll through a mental list of stuff for Annie, the pack and play, toys, monitor, all these little toddler necessities for survival that I must bring along and not forget and what if I do? I feel those shoulders tightening up, my jaw tensing and clenching, and stress taking hold.

I move fast. I move through her room, not really caring if I wake her or not, because I think that she will enjoy watching me get things together. That is the great thing about kids this age, they just go with the flow. Whichever direction you point them, you can get them going that way. But she sleeps, so sweet. As much as I hate what I am having to do, I know that I cannot stay here and I cannot keep living this life, this unhappily, with this man.

I wonder how I used to love him. I wonder, how can that change? I think, though, that those are not the things I should be dwelling on at this moment. I shift my thinking around. I start a little spell in my mind, one in which I reenact the blue circle of light and protection around Annie and around me, the same light, encircling us both, holding us close and protecting us and leading us, a circle of light in which nothing can harm us and we are safe.

I pause and look into her crib, at her beautiful little perfect body lying before me, and I resist touching her even though it is a restraint I have to fulfill with all my will. I am not ready to wake her, not yet. I hold the light around us and know that there is magic surrounding us. I know that I can teach her whatever is in my heart, as long as it is good and pure and true, and no one can take that from me. We are free to believe what we want to believe in this country, and we are free to choose who to be with. I am blessed in all those regards. More thankfulness fills my heart—thankfulness that I live in this country, thankfulness that this little girl will not face those social injustices that can befall women, thankful that she can choose to be a witch or choose to be an atheist or a Catholic or whatever she wants. It doesn't matter, and it's all OK. I'm thankful that it's all changing. For her.

My phone rings. Shit. I told Xander not to call. I grab it in my pocket and silence the ringer before I even get it out to see who is calling. It's Mary. Oh, great. It's not even seven in the morning and she is ready to pray with me, I'm sure—ready to talk to me about marriage. She probably has been up since four preparing to talk to me, agonizing and praying over what to say.

Slipping out of Annie's room and into the guest room, I answer it. I think I only answered it because I didn't want her to call the land line next.

"Hi, Mary."

"Oh, hi, Veronica," she says in her sweet voice, always a little on the old lady-ish side. "I hope that I didn't wake you?"

"No, no, I was up." *Up packing to leave your son.* I leave that part out.

"Listen, I talked to Peter last night and I just could not sleep thinking about you two! You have just got to pray together about this and start off your communicating that way."

I break in. "Don't you think that people have different ways of handling things?" I say, as gently as I can. "Us praying together isn't going to work right now. We can't even have the littlest conversation without fighting."

"Listen, Veronica, you need the Lord right now. You need him to bring you strength through this."

"Maybe I can find strength within myself."

"Now I want you to know, it can be very dangerous, reading about—" She sighs and pauses slightly, not sure if she can utter the next word. "—witchcraft. I have seen things like this before. It is a dark path and the wrong one to take, and a very dangerous path. This is not the way for you to go and it is definitely not the way for little Annie . . ."

I break in again. "How do you even know what I am studying or what I believe? You haven't even asked."

"I know that it is straying from the Lord!"

I find it funny that she and my brother used the exact same phrase. Could they have talked? Obviously. But I shake that thought away, save it for later, to chew on with Xander.

She is still talking. "And I know that I will not have my granddaughter exposed to that! I will do everything in my power to keep her safe from that!"

"Look, I am not trying to anger you. I am just saying that my spirituality is evolving, and I like some things that are probably off the beaten path a little bit."

"No!" I hear her voice, choking up. "No, Veronica, no, you have to work through this. It is up to you, it is up to the woman, to guide the spirituality of her husband, to help him and be there to support him . . ." She trails off.

I am shaking my head. "I need equality in a marriage, and I am not getting it here. This is an opportunity for Pete to . . ."

She suddenly interrupts me, incensed by that word, *opportunity*. She yells into the phone, not at all sounding little old lady-ish anymore. "What?!" she yells. "An *opportunity* for him?! Veronica, you should be ashamed of yourself! You should . . ."

And that's it. *Click*. That's all I am going to take of that. Although my heart is pounding, it feels good. I am not going to be told that I should be ashamed of myself. Maybe it isn't the ideal opportunity for Pete, but it is an opportunity none-theless—a chance to rise to the occasion and actually listen to a woman for a change, even when she might say something he doesn't want to hear.

But I see more clearly now how he has been raised, how he has been taught, and what has been instilled in him about marriage. It isn't his fault, necessarily, and I am not blaming her, either. It just is what it is. But once we are adults, shouldn't we be able to look past those things, especially as Americans? I am feeling quite patriotic this morning! Of course, in a liberal way, and I smile to myself at that.

I stride out of the room, my heart calming down a bit, and I see Pete stirring. I go into Annie's room and finish up her packing, hoping that I am not forgetting anything. I peep around the corner, seeing that Pete has gotten up and gone into the bathroom. Perfect. Down the stairs, to the car, pack and play in the trunk, her stuff in, all set there.

I open the door and my phone rings again. *Oh god, it's probably Mary again.* I silence it and see, to my great relief, that it's Xander. I answer and tell him that I will have to call him back.

"I just wanted to tell you that I'm leaving a key in the carport, under the watering can on the shelf. You can come and stay as long as you want."

That makes me smile. "A million thank-yous wouldn't be enough, X." I pause for a moment, not sure how to tell him how grateful I am.

"No, now you just get all your ducks in a row and get out of there."

"I have so much to tell you. I'll buy wine today, for tonight."

"Yes! Oh god, I can't wait to hear." He laughs. "And get some candles and pig's blood too."

I chuckle. "It's dragon's blood. And I'll get a quart. So get ready. OK. I gotta go."

I can hear his smile. "All right. I love you."

"I love you, too."

I hear Annie, officially awake now, and I run up the stairs, watching my dirty black ballet flats skip every other step. I peek into her room. She is standing up, stinking and smiling and looking precious.

After another morning with a disgusting diaper which I hope is not a sign of things to come, but suspect it is, I get her all ready and dressed and comfy cute. I shove the diaper down into the Diaper Genie and leave it. Pete can deal with emptying that. Although another premonition strikes me— that I will still be the one doing all these things when we start to sell the house.

I stand and look at her precious room for a moment, with its striped walls and delicate little chandelier, and I remember that girl, the one who set up this room and expected life to be so different after the birth of this child. That girl, me, was right. Things did get different. But things never seem to change in quite the way we expect. I think back, and I remember being quite fearful, scared of what it would be like to be a mother, despite the fact that gazillions of women who came before me, my ancestral mothers, had all done it, too. That should have given me confidence, but I truly had none as a mother, as a woman, as a wife. That confidence was only now coming, once I proved to myself what I was capable of and what I could actually do.

Now there's this new experience, something I didn't dream that I could tackle. A new level of confidence is approaching, and the fear is very slowly leaving me, being replaced by confidence, even if it is in a molasses-like fashion.

I think back to that person I envisioned, the one who has seemed, at moments, so far away, and I think about how this is what she has to do. She must get herself out of a situation in which she is this unhappy. I know she has to do it with her chin up and no regrets, being careful and keeping her head cool. I want to be her. I want it so badly.

I hold Annie tightly and step carefully down the eighteen stairs toward the first floor. Pete is out of the bathroom now, looking at us, beginning to talk sweetly to Annie. He reaches for her, and I hand her to him.

I dare not say anything about leaving when he has her. I have to be holding her, I have to have her with me, because to leave here without her would mean something awful to me, like *Kramer vs. Kramer*, the mother leaving, the societal implications of which I hate. The idea of Pete telling people that I left him and Annie will not do at all. I think of the flip, that I left him and took Annie from him and the sob story that he can attach to that one—but at least I have her, at least I have that little something intact. I know that I will be the bad guy. I know that I will have stories attached to me. Pete will hate me and so will a lot of people, but that woman in the future? She's too big for all that. She's too secure and handles things well. While I know that I will still be human and still hurt over things, I know that she is with me. I feel relieved that I can imagine her once again, that she seems close once again.

My heart always softens when I see him with her. I think he knows this and sees it written on my face. He holds her and is sweet to her. I remember the man who has yelled and snapped at me, and the two people seem worlds apart. It's funny to me how the same person can have so many facets. It has always been strange to me. Sometimes it is hard to reconcile those people together, but it is a reminder to me that even the worst person must have some good aspects.

I always enjoy movies like *L.A. Confidential,* in which no one is all bad or all good, because it seems more realistic and more like the way human beings really behave. We all have our bad and our good. Even Mary, who I am sure many people would and probably do describe as a saint, does.

But then, maybe even saints have their off moments. God knows witches do.

I tell Pete good morning.

"Good morning," he replies curtly.

"I hung up on your mom this morning." I pause. Stone-faced, I add, "Sorry. But you'll probably hear about that."

He gives his little laugh of disbelief and shakes his head, like I am so very unbelievable and immature. He doesn't pursue the conversation, and I am glad.

I make Annie breakfast and go through those old motions, hopefully for the last time in this particular place in my life. I let Pete play with her and enjoy this time, knowing that it won't last long. He usually peters out fairly quickly. Sometimes I think it's all for show, to me or to himself, or maybe to both, I'm not sure.

I call Annie for breakfast, and he brings her over. I feed her on autopilot, especially this morning, when my mind is anywhere but here. It's like I am here but I am not here, trying to stay present for these last few moments but trying to work out how I will leave.

I have a moment when I think that he could just go upstairs, hole up in his office, and I could pop Annie in the car. We could drive away, and that would be that—we'd be gone. But that seems to miss the point. It seems wrong on some level. I have no idea what I am going to say, but I do know that the engine will be running and Annie will be in her car seat, garage door open, gun ready to fire for the race to start.

He does just what I thought he would. He heads up to his office, to presumably work, and I sit there, wondering what happens next. I wish I could ask that future me, that strong version of myself. So I do. I close my eyes as Annie plays with some Cheerios on her high chair. I see myself talking to future me, both of us sitting in comfortable chairs, like my brown chenille one upstairs, across from each other. The rest of the place is dark and nondescript nothingness.

I start asking.

"What do I do? What do I say?"

"You just have to stay strong and sure of yourself. Keep this little girl in mind. Keep her interests at heart."

"But what if he gets mad, yells at me, calls me all kinds of things?"

"Is that really anything new? And is that where you want to be, anyway? Wouldn't that just confirm that you are doing the right thing, choosing the right path?"

"What if he cries, falls on the floor, and begs me to stay?" (I think this, but I also think it's preposterous. But just in case, what if?)

"*Then you tell him, if it means that much, that your needs are not getting met. You two can talk about it in the future and see if those needs can get met, if you can be fulfilled as a person and as a woman, but for now, you need some space. Don't be afraid to ask for what you need.*"

"*Wow, you're smart. Are you really me?*"

She smiles.

 *Thirteen*

GRAB YOUR BROOM, IT'S TIME TO FLY.

So I get it all ready. I open the garage door. I look at the packed car as I load Annie in. I start the car and have it all in line, and I know that this is it.

I go back inside, setting foot across that saltillo tile. While I know it isn't the last time, I do know that it is the last time with me living under this roof, with me maintaining the façade of this life and this marriage with Pete. His family is going to freak out. This makes me a tiny bit happy. It's twisted and wrong, I know, but there it is.

I step to underneath the stairs and I take a breath, knowing that once I call him, I have to follow through. I can't take the easy way out. This is my last chance to drive away, my last chance to leave and not talk to him and just drive.

I consider leaving a note for a moment, but I have an aversion to putting things in writing. It's evidence. It can come back and bite you in the ass later, when you least expect it. So that's out. Of course, it could just say, "We're going," or something simple like that, and I think that might even be what I am about to say. I reach down and pet the fuzzy white puppy head below my knees. What about these guys? These furry babies? I give my head a slight shake and tell myself I will worry about them later.

I breathe more deeply and call Pete's name. He yells back from behind the closed door of his office. I can't hear him.

"Can you come down here?"

"Hang on," he replies, a slightly annoyed tone in his voice.

I hear rustling and papers and things banging and clanging around. He opens the door hard and looks down at me from the landing, speaking very tersely and looking down his nose at me, from high above. His lordship utters, tightly, with a stone set in his eyes, "What's up?"

I ask again. "Can you come down here for a minute?"

He gives a long breath out of his nose. "Well, *what is it?*"

Maybe this is supposed to happen here. He clearly doesn't want to come down, doesn't want to do anything I ask of him—probably a foreshadowing of things to come. Maybe that is OK. Maybe we don't need that garage to be the scene of all our goodbyes or worst moments together, the site of all my bombshells.

So I decide to do it now.

"We're leaving."

"OK," he nonchalantly says with a shrug of his hands.

"No. *Leaving.*"

I see him swallow. "Excuse me?" He tries to use politeness to hide his welling anger.

He starts down the stairs. I move toward the garage door at a matched pace.

"I am leaving this house, and taking Annie for now, and we can work out a schedule later on when you can take her and when I can take her."

"You're leaving." He gives the laugh. I can see the anger in his eyes, see it in his reddening complexion. He sticks his lips out slightly and looks out the window of the front door, then says, "That figures. Just running away, huh?"

"I am too unhappy to stay. I am just not . . . getting . . . what I need here." I hear the trepidation in my voice. This sounded so much better coming from my future self. I try to summon some of those things she told me. *What were they again? Um, strength? Caution?*

His anger incites anew. "You are not taking my daughter out of this house and not even letting me know where you are taking her!"

My hand is on the open garage door and I cross the threshold, into the garage, and check that Annie is OK. I can see through the tinted glass and the reflections that she is playing with a toy, content and fine. Relief. I move toward the loaded, running car and try to keep my head on straight. *Oh yeah, that was one of the things future me said to try to do!*

I reply calmly. "We are going to stay at Xander's. He has two extra bedrooms, and Annie will be fine. Call me later, and we can work out a schedule, like I said."

I can tell he doesn't like this at all, and it is hitting him that it is really happening. "Have you even got her things?"

"Of course, I do." Both of us are speaking in calmer tones.

His face is a mix of confusion, anger, and sadness. I don't think he knows which way to go. I am rooting for the confusion and the sadness to win out, even though the anger would make me more justified to leave. I wait to see what is going to happen. A neighbor walks by, someone we don't know, walking their dog. I know that we are both thankful that it isn't someone we know, someone who might try to stop and chit-chat. We both turn our heads to look. I hold the car door between us, carefully gliding one foot into the floorboard.

He makes his emotional choice. It's sadness.

Tears fill his eyes. They turn red, and his lips tense up into a face that breaks my heart. My shoulders sag, and I don't know what to do.

"Please, please, Veronica, don't do this!" He chokes back tears through his voice.

"I'm sorry, Pete, but I have to . . ."

My throat gets tight for a second, and I feel a heat rising up my face. There's a small burst of energy spurred on by emotion. That familiar little voice of doubt wants to break in, but I shake my head. *No.* I shake it again and again until all I can feel is the movement. I take a deep breath. I can cry later. I take another deep breath. I can and probably will cry later. It can all come out later. But now is not the time. I reach in and draw upon that feeling I had when I cast the first spell—the strength I know that lies within, the strength to live my story, speak my truth, and pass it on to my child. That is the spell that we all have within us. That is our own magic. That is where I go now and where I must stay.

He breaks in. "No, you don't. I'm begging you. I'll do anything, just please, please don't do this."

I wonder how much of this is really wanting me to stay and how much of this is about saving face in front of family and neighbors and friends. I am sure that he is having those thoughts, those *What will I tell everyone?* thoughts.

But I feel bad, a jolt of fault and blame, and I think it is wrong to doubt his motives. There probably is a very scared and sad part of him, wanting me to stay, wanting his daughter right here with him.

I reach out to hug him, while staying steeled to my decisions, because I really don't know what else to do. He stiffly pulls away, wiping the tears from below his lids. He knows I am going to do this, no matter what.

I think back to what I was going to tell him if this happened.

"If you are truly willing to do anything, then you'll have to show me. Over time we might be able to work something out." But as I say this, I can see that to him, it is all about this moment. It is all right here, and if I leave, then I am not giving him the chance. But I know that, from my perspective, I don't believe that anything will change if we stay. I don't believe that he means it. It all rings false to me. It is just about saving face, about me not leaving.

He shakes his head and snorts through his nose. We both know what is happening, and although it means different things in both our worlds, it means the same thing, too.

"I'll just talk to you later," I say delicately. He stares out into the cul-de-sac, blankly. I get in the car and am so glad that this part of it is almost done.

I put the car in reverse and once again, I see him standing there, left in the garage. I know that I have to go forward, that I have to pursue finding that future self, that stronger version of me, that truer woman, that witch who knows herself and loves herself too much to deny who she really is.

I feel sad, and I feel happy. I feel all the emotions rush into me and mix together. I drive with a smile and tears, with a sadness for things left behind; I drive forward, moving toward whatever it is the future holds, knowing that as long as I can see that future strong woman, I will be all right, and so will Annie.

Acknowledgments

Huge thanks to Brooke Warner and Samantha Strom for their dedication and patience in helping me get this project finished. A special thank you to everyone at She Writes Press for their help, too. My Moon Sisters— Bijou, Astra, and Clementine— thank you for what you have each given and shown me in my own becoming. To my friends and family, thank you for your support. It means the world to me. And I never would have even started this project without first encountering NaNoWriMo, so thank you to them for the push I needed so many years ago.

And one other thing: remember that you can be anything you dream of. If you read this novel and think to yourself, "Hey, I could write something like that"—you can! Go for it. You are a rock star, and it's never, ever too late to make your dreams into reality.

About the Author

AMY EDWARDS is a rock musician, radio personality, author, actress, personal coach, speaker and podcast host, as well as a mom to two girls. From her home in Austin, Texas, she is also the co-author of the children's book *Starla and the Boogie Deluxe* (Archway, 2019). She will co-host her new affirmations podcast, "Go Aff Yourself," launching in 2019. Amy's musical work with her band Amy and the Hi-Fis includes "Ghosts and Saints" (2014); "FORWARD" (2014); "Get LIVE" (2015); "Superstar," (2016); "Little Birds" (2017); and the double album "Magic, Vols. 1 & 2" (2018). Learn more at www.amyedwards.com.

Author photo © Paige Elizabeth Casey

Selected Titles from She Writes Press

She Writes Press is an independent publishing company founded to serve women writers everywhere. Visit us at www.shewritespress.com.

Center Ring by Nicole Waggoner. $17.95, 978-1-63152-034-1. When a startling confession rattles a group of tightly knit women to its core, the friends are left analyzing their own roads not taken and the vastly different choices they've made in life and love.

Play for Me by Céline Keating. $16.95, 978-1-63152-972-6. Middle-aged Lily impulsively joins a touring folk-rock band, leaving her job and marriage behind in an attempt to find a second chance at life, passion, and art.

The Black Velvet Coat by Jill G. Hall. $16.95, 978-1-63152-009-9. When the current owner of a black velvet coat—a San Francisco artist in search of inspiration—and the original owner, a 1960s heiress who fled her affluent life fifty years earlier, cross paths, their lives are forever changed . . .for the better.

In the Heart of Texas by Ginger McKnight-Chavers. $16.95, 978-1-63152-159-1. After spicy, forty-something soap star Jo Randolph manages in twenty-four hours to burn all her bridges in Hollywood, along with her director/boyfriend's beach house, she spends a crazy summer back in her West Texas hometown—and it makes her question whether her life in the limelight is worth reclaiming.

A Work of Art by Micayla Lally. $16.95, 978-1631521683. After their break-up—and different ways of dealing with it—Julene and Samson eventually find their way back to each other, but when she finds out what he did to keep himself busy while they were apart, she wonders: Can she trust him again?

Wishful Thinking by Kamy Wicoff. $16.95, 978-1-63152-976-4. A divorced mother of two gets an app on her phone that lets her be in more than one place at the same time, and quickly goes from zero to hero in her personal and professional life—but at what cost?